THE EMBROIDERED COUCH

繡榻野史

繡榻野史

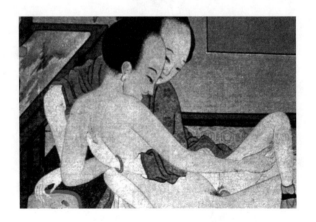

LÜ TIANCHENG

THE EMBROIDERED COUCH

Translated from the Chinese
with an Introduction by
LENNY HU

ARSENAL PULP PRESS
Vancouver

THE EMBROIDERED COUCH
English translation copyright © 2001 by Lenny Hu

ARSENAL PULP PRESS
103-1014 Homer Street
Vancouver, B.C.
Canada V6B 2W9
arsenalpulp.com

The publisher gratefully acknowledges the support of the Canada Council for the Arts and the British Columbia Arts Council for its publishing program, and the Government of Canada through the Book Publishing Industry Development Program for its publishing activities.

Cover design by Lisa Eng-Lodge
Interior design by Solo
Cover illustration courtesy of the collection of Xue Yanqun
Printed and bound in Canada

CANADIAN CATALOGUING IN PUBLICATION DATA:
Lü, Tiancheng, 1580-
  The embroidered couch

  ISBN 1-55152-101-6

I.Hu, Lenny. II. Title.
PL2698.L853E42 2001   895.1'346   C2001-911279-3

for my mentor
R. W. L. Guisso

ACKNOWLEDGMENTS

First of all, I wish to take this opportunity to thank all those eminent translators and scholars of Ming-Qing fiction, especially Patrick Hanan, David T. Roy, and David Hawks, from whose works I have greatly benefited.

In making this book, I have been helped by several friends and teachers. Professor R.W.L. Guisso and Mr. Martin Hunter read the first portion of the manuscript and gave me much encouragement. Dr. Kwok-yu Wong spent a lot of time for me looking up the names of historical figures in his reference books and Dr. David Zhou, as always, graciously offered me his invaluable aid in helping solve my computer problems. The famous artist Xue Yanqun lent me his own Ming erotic pictures, one of which has been chosen as the artwork for the cover.

I owe a special debt to Professor Wendy Larson of the University of Oregon, who read my translation from the beginning to the end with minute care and made quite a few changes or suggestions for stylistic improvement. At my request she kindly retranslated the three tongue-twisters for me. Due to our different personal styles, however, I have only partially, not entirely, adopted her renditions, for which I feel very sorry. I hope she can forgive me.

Finally, I would also like to thank my editor Linda Field for her careful editing, and Brian Lam for the publication of this book as well as everything he has done for it.

INTRODUCTION

The Embroidered Couch, like many other late Ming erotic works, was originally published under a pseudonym. The title page of the novel ascribed the authorship to a Master "Perverse Love." Thanks to Wang Jide, we now know that the author's real name was Lü Tiancheng. In the fourth volume of his *Qulü* (Rules For the Libretto), Wang made the following remarks:

> Qingzhi [i.e., Lü Tiancheng] is a prolific author, uniquely skilled in depicting romantic love and salacious scenes. The well-known *The Embroidered Couch* and *Leisure Enjoyment* were both his works, written for fun in his youth.

Some scholars have taken what he said with a handful of salt. Yet since Wang was a contemporary of Lü, he must have talked on good ground and this, I suggest, can be confirmed through careful reading of the novel. The novel sets its background in Yangzhou, and it also refers to some other real places, such as Nanjing, Changzhou, Guazhou, and Huzhou, all of which were in Jiangsu and Zhejiang. These two provinces were where Lü Tiancheng was born and brought up, and where he spent most of his time on academic and literary pursuits from early adulthood to his untimely death. The main and pivotal supports for his authorship come, assuredly, from two historical figures the novel mentions. The famous courtesan Ma Xianglan, who was active in Nanjing in the middle of the Wanli reign (around 1600) and died soon afterward, is one; the other is Emperor Shenzong's son, the Prince of Fujian, born in 1582 and notoriously known as a "Transgressive Young Man of the Propriety" for contending for the heir apparency that was finally, in 1601, given his elder brother Changluo (for details, see Note 20). As persons of note, they provide important factual evidence – the approximate date of when *The Embroidered Couch* was written. Determining the exact year has proved difficult, but we can at least infer that *Couch* could not have been completed earlier than 1600 and later than 1610, a time frame precisely conforming to Wang's claim that Lü wrote this work "in his youth."

Lü Tiancheng, whose style was Qinzhi and whose sobriquet was Yulansheng, was born in 1580 and died before 1618. A son of a scholar-gentry family in Yuyao county, Zhejiang province, he passed, in his teens, the first level of the Civil Service Examinations, getting the Licentiate degree. But it seems that he never succeeded in the Provincial Examination, nor did he, with only brief service as a minor official in the Nanjing government, rise far out of poverty. His grandmother, Madam Sun, was a bibliophile who had a large collection of popular literature that was particularly rich in drama. Strongly influenced by her, Lü, too, was very fond of script writing and for a long time studied under Shen Jing (1533-1610), the leading playwright of the Wujiang School. During his short life span, so far as we know, he wrote eight *zaju* plays and fifteen *chuanqi* plays altogether, yet none but one have survived. He has also left us with a two-volume book of dramatic criticism, *Qüpin* (Characterizations of Plays), which has become an indispensable work for scholars specializing in drama of the Ming dynasty, especially in its theatrical theory.

The Embroidered Couch, written by Lü as a young man, was the "most licentious and inflaming book" of his age. It achieved immediate acceptance after publication and was exceptionally popular in the circle of literati (the scholar Vesperus in *Carnal Prayer Mat*, an erotic novel published a few decades later, enlightens his newly-wedded wife on sexual pleasures by deliberately giving her some renowned "pornographic" books to read, among which is *Couch*). Yet whatever eclat it might have enjoyed in its heyday, to modern readers it has become obscure, and is even more obscure in the West. As Patrick Hanan puts it:

> Few people [in the West] realize that a
> lively tradition of erotic fiction existed
> in China, particularly in the sixteenth
> and seventeenth centuries. (Introduction
> to *Carnal Prayer Mat*)

Its falling into oblivion was, no doubt, attributable to the interdictions imposed on erotica after the Manchus took power in China in 1644. In the twenty-sixth year of the Kangxi reign (1688), an imperial decree was promulgated to the effect that "all the fiction with obscene words must be immediately destroyed and will never again be allowed for publication." This decree was re-issued in 1702 and then in 1710, and was finally legalized in the *Da Qing luling* (The Legal Codes of the Qing). In the nineteenth century even the local government began to take harsh action on so-called problematic books and *The Embroidered Couch* was banned a number of times, first by the Prefect of Huzhou in 1838, then by the Governor of Zhejiang in 1844, and the last time by Ding Richang, the Governor of Jiangsu, in 1868. It continued its subterranean existence in the twentieth century, kept alive only surreptitiously by some research libraries. Up to the present day, it remains a book much deplored by Chinese critics. *Zhongguo xiaoshuo baike quanshu* (Encyclopaedia of the Traditional Chinese Fiction), which was published in recent years in Beijing, introduces the novel with such a critique: "[This work], with its focus exclusively on sexual intercourse, was an adverse current in late Ming fiction."

If somebody asks me, "What is the most distinguishing feature of *The Embroidered Couch* in comparison with other late Ming sexual fiction?" I will reply without hesitation, "Unashamed licentiousness." *The Embroidered Couch* was published at the spring tide of Chinese erotic literature, perhaps just a year or two after the free circulation of *Jin Ping Mei* (The Golden Lotus), so it clearly bears a visible resemblance to its much acclaimed precursor in subject matter and technique, and even in the way of naming its main characters (for example, the female protagonist Jin and the male protagonist Easterngate in the novel were obviously named after Jinlian and Westerngate in *Jin Ping Mei*). However, it differs radically in two ways: it is more consciously lascivious in its employment of subliterary sex terms, and at the same time, it is much bolder in its description of carnal activities, largely of the deviant type.

Let us look at its language first. It is impossible, I think, that in the fiction of the previous centuries we can find ribaldry in any way resembling Lü Tiancheng's. Admittedly, the use of filthy words started with *Jin Ping Mei*, yet it is confined to the most intense moments when Golden Lotus shouts abuse at someone, and its narrative style, even in presenting the graphic details of copulation, is kept wilfully elegant. *The Embroidered Couch*, however, is distinctly different. The author shows an unusually strong preference for vulgarism. Words like "cock" and "cunt" almost entirely replace those euphemistic equivalents (e.g., "jade stalk" and "female orifice"), becoming a keynote of the novel. They are not only a working vocabulary of the narrator, but are integrated into the language used by the characters in their daily sexual life. Men, in making love, feel unabashed in talking dirty, and so do women. Even the well-cultured lady Madam Ma will unwittingly burst out, being atingle when Jin inserts a vibrator into her vagina, "Indeed, this cock is not bad!" This generous use of lubricious diction, undoubtedly more faithful to real life in the portrayal of its coarse and erogenic aspects, relates Lü's novel to its very modern Western counterparts.

A second characteristic is the forbidden territory it explores. What we see in *Jin Ping Mei* is basically adulteries, the adulteries between Westerngate and his women. When we read *The Embroidered Couch*, however, we seem to have come back into a world of our own, a contemporary world in which we are able to meet gays, lesbians, and bisexuals, and in which masturbation, *menage à trois*, and incest (or "pseudo-incest," to use Andrew Plaks' term) are quite a common sight. Adultery is still an intriguing activity, yet it is no longer cryptic the way it is with the pleasure-seeker and his mistresses in *Jin Ping Mei*. It is, instead, permitted and encouraged by the voluntarily "cuckolded" husband. At the beginning Jin and Dali do not dare openly carry on before Easterngate, despite their burning passion for each other. The novel then takes considerable space in describing how the husband goads and tantalizes his wife. "'Although I call him [Dali] Younger Brother,' said Easterngate to Jin, 'he is actually my partner, just like you. You are both my bedmates, so what's your embarrassment about?'" After having finished his persuading work, he helps Jin wash her privates and then escorts her personally to the outer study, where Dali has been awaiting her for a long time. Later, in like manner, occurs the unusual liaison between Easterngate and Madam Ma, a liaison schemed, arranged, and shared from the very beginning to the end by a third person – the fornicator's wife.

The late Ming was a very libertarian epoch, similar to the ideologically open era we now live in, and the Lower Yangtze delta was then the most economically advanced and culturally prosperous region, where converged the aspiring and most radical literati of the country. No wonder that Lü Tiancheng, born in such a time and raised in such an environment, with impulsive vigour and brilliant talent, could produce so bold a work. *The Embroidered Couch* is not a "crazy" fabrication as some people have accused. On the contrary, it is a mirror reflecting the libertinism of the *fin de siècle*.

This, perhaps, is where the historical significance of the novel lies. In the book on Ling Mengchu's (1580-1644) erotic stories (in collaboration with R. W. L. Guisso, forthcoming), I wrote:

> If we are incapable of imagining any new pleasures in this world, we can at least enjoy a different kind of pleasure: "pleasure in the truth of pleasure." (See Foucault, *History of Sexuality*, vol. 1, p. 71.) Without this "truth of pleasure," could we fully understand why Robert van Gulik says that after the Manchus conquered China in 1644 (this is where he concludes his *Sexual Life in Ancient China*), "there occurred

profound changes in the Chinese attitude
to sex"? And could we fully understand
how these "profound changes" have been
related to the process of Chinese history?

(The attitude of Chinese people toward sex has, since the
Qing dynasty, greatly changed. We could not have imagined,
if not for late Ming erotica, that China had undergone a sex-
ually-modern stage at the turn of the seventeenth century!)

Yet *The Embroidered Couch* has never achieved any real crit-
ical recognition, and I am fully aware that pointing out its
historical value alone might not be convincing enough to
those who doubt that it has literary merits. It is really, I
admit, not easy to separate it from hack pornography
because of its subject matter. But anybody who has read
this novel without taking a moral aversion to its content
would probably agree with me that it is first of all a fine
work of mimesis, or, a framing novel of manners within
which is enclosed a lurid story of sexual adventures. True,
it has some typical qualities of erotic fiction: the exaggera-
tion of penis size, the extravagant quantification of sex, and
the hypersexuality of women. Yet on the whole it is authen-
tic and true to life. It relates an interesting tale of the wanton and incestuous sex activities in two gentry families, and
in so doing, faithfully and with succintness and ease,
describes how the cynical protagonist, with an ennui common
in an age when "conformist" morality was disintegrating,
seeks new, extraordinary erotic stimulation: excitement,
pain, and jealousy in experiencing perversity, complicated
entanglements in which he gets involved after much exhil-
arating enjoyment, and finally, disillusionment and renun-
ciation of earthly joys, and transcendence and the attainment of spiritual fruition of a Buddhistic type.

The late Ming saw the flourishing of fiction: never had any previous age produced so great an amount of novels, novellas, and short stories as in that period. Nevertheless, there was none so daringly realistic, so straightforward and stark-naked in depicting the decadence of scholars, nor was there any work that mixes the wildness of comedy and the pathos of tragedy and combines the fabulous sex and the genuine feeling, so skillfully and so refinedly as to be compared to *Couch*.

Lü seems to have possessed a very unique gift which has hardly been noticed by his adverse critics. He could, through the elaborately designed plot and dramatized dialogue, create life-like and idiosyncratic characters in a limited space. Easterngate, for instance, is a liberal-minded but henpecked husband who can do nothing substantial to control his wife, letting her have an affair with his homosexual partner; Dali is a naïve youth, docile and with real affection; Jin appears a vixen, lecherous and shrewd, but at the same time very capable and reasonable; and Madam Ma is a well-cultivated widow, sincere and candid, yet easily swayed by her emotions. Each of them strikes us as a vivid and different individual with his or her own temperament. Even minor persona exhibit their singularity. Saihong the slave girl, whose recalcitrance and invidious rivalry are well rendered through carefully chosen details such as her refusal to sleep with Easterngate and her beating the fellow maid Little Pretty, provides us with a brilliant illustration in this respect. (This outstanding talent of Lü's we can see again, only three hundred years later, in Lu Xun's short stories.)

Of course, *The Embroidered Couch* has some weaknesses. The process of intercourse is at times too lengthy and the denoument seems hasty, covering in a few pages the entire course of what Easterngate undergoes in several years — from the ruin of his family to his tonsure and final enlightenment. We cannot blame the retribution plot: it seems a natural and reasonable continuity for the "hero" (or anti-hero) who, after much pleasure-seeking and merry-making, gets bored and wants to repent and be punished. It is only that his repentance and punishment come too quickly, and in too hurried a tempo, to be more than a mere didactic apocalypse. Was this part finished by the author himself in a rush or was it added by someone else, for example, the "proofreader" whose name appears on the title page? I cannot make a judgment on the basis of the Chinese versions I have seen.

This is the first translation of the novel in any Western language. It is imperfect, to be sure, and may also contain mistakes I myself am unaware of. I only hope that readers will come away with some sense of having had a delightful taste, and that they will give me their generous advice for my further revision.

L.L.H.
Surrey, BC
December 2000

繡榻野史

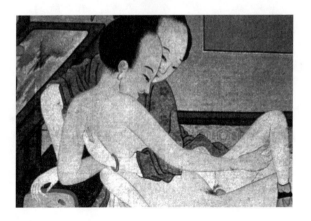

THE EMBROIDERED COUCH

Part I

Old anecdotes about this sort of thing are plenty,
And I'll not write one more piece in elegant phraseology.
To present a life-like scene of unusual love is surely not easy,
And it might also be too provocative to bear comfortably.

All suffered because they gave rein to illicit adultery,
So it isn't terrific to get involved in a lecherous activity.
Here is advice for men and women having a prurient proclivity:
Don't overindulge till death comes and all becomes empty.

— to the tune of *The Moon on the Western River*

Our story goes that in Yangzhou there was a licentiate surnamed Yao with the personal name Tongxin. Since he lived in the district of Eastern Gate, he gave himself a sobriquet: the Scholar of Easterngate.

Easterngate was an erudite, well-read and also familiar with Buddhist hows and whys. He enjoyed writing tasteless doggerels and often hung around with courtesans in brothels. He was by nature an unconventional romantic gentleman.

He first married a daughter of the Wei family. Both of them were born in the same year, *jiazi* [1564]. His wife was ugly and always felt out of sorts, unable to give him what he needed when it came to sex. She died at the age of twenty-five. Easterngate regretted his ungratifying former marriage and was determined to find a beautiful woman to be his future wife.

There was another licentiate, a juvenile named Zhao Dali. He was twelve years younger than Easterngate and was handsome and lovely. Easterngate did all he could, and by hook or by crook finally succeeded in cajoling him into sleeping with him. In the daytime they were brothers, while at night they made love as if they were husband and wife. Though Easterngate had lost his spouse, the vacuum left by her death was fortunately filled by Dali's ass.

Several years passed. Now Easterngate was twenty-eight.

One day a matchmaker surnamed Sun came visiting him, telling him that a Jin family, the owner of the silk and satin store located on the west side of the Nunnery of Jade Flower in an adjacent street, had a beautiful daughter, white-skinned and delicate, who had just turned nineteen. Easterngate was delighted to hear the news. He prepared a rich betrothal gift and had it sent to her house, and then on a selected auspicious day, married her. When he saw his bride, he found that she was indeed a knockout, peerless and unique. He was rapt with joy. He was told, after making some inquiries about her, that his wife had often carried on with menservants before she married. But he did not care much about such things.

He was reluctant to part company with Dali even during his honeymoon days. Dali called on him every day and no one else paid much attention to his visits.

Dali's mother was surnamed Ma, whom people called Madam Ma. Madam Ma was a widow whose husband had died when she was only twenty. She taught Dali to read and write and kept him under strict control. She was well-disciplined herself, and Dali, being an obedient son, complied with her every wish.

In the year *guisi* [1594], Easterngate was thirty, Jin was twenty-one, Dali was eighteen. Madam Ma, who had given birth to Dali at the age of sixteen, was now thirty-three. She intended to look for a beautiful girl for her son, but Dali said he wanted to concentrate on his studies to prepare for the Civil Service Examinations, not quite ready yet for marriage. With her permission to study outside with a friend, he continued his reading with Easterngate, returning home to see his mother every other day.

Easterngate often spent nights with his Younger Brother in the outer study. That made the two men become all the more intimate. Dali, staying there all day long, caught glimpses of Jin from time to time. He was deeply infatuated with her.

What a beautiful woman! he thought. How can I have her in my arms and enjoy her to my heart's content?

Seeing this handsome youth, Jin also lusted after him.

"How lovely this young scholar is!" she said to herself. "I wish I could just eat him up in one big bite!"

They admired each other, sneaking amorous glances whenever possible. Easterngate caught some wind of their itchings, yet he loved his wife dearly and decided to let them fool around as much as they liked. He hated himself for having injured his health in adolescent overindulgence, and now, being an older man, he no longer had good staying prowess. Since Dali was his most intimate friend, he thought: I may as well let him have a tryst with her. That might give me some different pleasures.

One day the two men were drinking and eating together. Easterngate went in to invite Jin to join them for dinner. She shook her head, reluctant to dine with them.

"I would feel embarrassed. Better not to ask me to keep him company," she declined.

Easterngate laughed. "Although I call him Younger Brother, he is actually my partner, just like you. You are both my bedmates, so what's your embarrassment about?"

"You two may have had some intimate relations," Jin said, concealing her chucklings with her hand, "but what has that to do with me? How can I sit with him at the same table?"

"Come on!" said Easterngate. "Don't be so finicky."

Jin had no alternative but to come out for dinner. Thereafter they ate meals together every day. On the day the three of them were together drinking, celebrating Easterngate's birthday, Dali and Jin sank into a burning lust, ogling each other constantly. Dali deliberately dropped his chopsticks on the floor, and bending down to pick them up, gave her a pinch on the top of her foot. Jin responded with a smile, and then took a red berry, bit half of it and put the other half on the table. Dali stealthily stuffed it into his mouth as Easterngate looked away. Jin broke into giggles. They did not part company until after the feast had dispersed in the evening.

In spite of their growing intimacy, there were after all some obstacles not easily surmountable. Easterngate had no secluded room in his house; however hard they racked their brains, they could create no opportunity to carry on a secret assignation by themselves.

One day Easterngate was in the study talking to Dali about his romances when he suddenly slapped the desk, exclaiming, "I wish I could enjoy some wonderful time screwing the most beautiful woman in the world!"

"Sister-in-Law is very beautiful," said Dali. "Why do you trouble to look for someone else, Elder Brother? Are you not satisfied with your happy life? Or you have grown tired of meat and want to have some vegetables for a change?"

"Sister-in-Law was indeed very pretty when she married me," Easterngate admitted, "but now she doesn't look so wonderfully attractive."

"To me, she is still beautiful," Dali said, "and I can't find another woman as beautiful as she is."

Easterngate guffawed. "Younger Brother, you are praising her for her good looks, so you might have a hankering for her yourself?"

Dali grinned. "She is my sister-in-law. Even if I do have a hankering for her, what can I do about it?"

"That's easy to arrange," Easterngate declared. "You know in history Cangwurao married a woman, and since she was beautiful, he gave her to his elder brother.[1] I can also do so, giving my wife to Younger Brother!"

Dali was stirred. "Elder Brother, if you do as Cangwurao did, I'll surely follow Chen Ping![2] But what would Sister-in-Law think of it?"

"Women are of easy virtue," said Easterngate. "To be frank with you, Sister-in-Law would perhaps be even more eager than you. Just sleep in this study tonight as you usually do, and I'll invite her out."

Upon hearing this, Dali hurriedly bowed twice. "Elder Brother," he said, "you are so kind-hearted! I'm willing to let you ride anal whenever you want to. Even if you pound my asshole into the shape of a barrel, I'd not say a word. I'm really grateful to you. Now, allow me to go home to see my mother. I'll be back soon."

He took his leave and went trotting off.

Easterngate came into the bedroom. Jin had eaten her supper and was about to undress for sleep. Easterngate gave her a kiss on the mouth.

"Has Dali left?" she asked.

"Yes," Easterngate said. "Just now he told me tales of his erotic exploits, making me feel horny. Could you please remove your clothes and open your legs quick? I need a good thrust to work me off."

"This is a matter between us," said Jin. "Is there any need to get incentive from somebody else?"

She removed her pants and lay back on a chair, with her thighs spread apart. Then she grabbed hold of his erection and guided it inside. Easterngate started bucking and pumping in no time.

"What did Dali say about sex that has made you so aroused?" Jin inquired, grinning. "I would also like to hear it, to get high."

"In the beginning," said Easterngate, "he complained that my object was too big as I played with him, and he also made a fuss about my long diddling. But now, two years later, his rod has grown even larger than mine. He boasts he has a lot of tricks and is able to keep from ejaculating all night. All the women he slept with, he says, ended up with a swollen and ripped-up pussy. In Changzhou[3] there was a tart with an unusual knack. She could lock a prick in her cunt and no well-hung man was able to give her a hundred strokes without unleashing spurts of semen. But Dali did her a full night. By the fifth watch she was nearly dead. Yet he didn't release her until after she cried out for mercy."

Jin smiled. "The shameless slut courted trouble, so she could only blame herself for that," she said.

"But Dali's huge dick is indeed stunning," Easterngate stressed. "I myself can't but give a cheer upon seeing it, not to mention women. It measures a good 8.3 inches in length and four inches strong in diameter.[4] It's hard as an iron club and hot as burning fire. Had my late wife still been alive, I bet she would have urged him to go competing with Xue Aocao."[5]

With this he gave her a hug.

"Honey, get your loose pit screwed by him and you'll taste a real pleasure."

Jin felt a thrill of arousal.

"Oh, please don't say it any more," she exhaled. "My bones are melting. If he is really that good as you are boasting, just let me deal with him. I'll see if he can conquer me."

"Fine," said Easterngate. "I'll ask him to come later this

evening and sleep with you in the study. Would this be an agreeable arrangement for you?"

She nodded, her eyes remaining closed.

"I'm dying," she moaned.

"Since you love him so dearly, honey, why haven't you tried to date him before?" asked Easterngate.

"Hey," Jin countered, "you brought up this topic, so how could you say that I love him? I may love him, but I love you as well. I don't know how I can share my love of you with somebody else."

Easterngate smiled. "Look, he is my most affectionate partner and you are my most cherished wife, so it's quite natural for you both to love each other. I'll invite him over right away. Just make sure you do your best and beat the shit out of him. Tomorrow I'll laugh at him. He needs to be taught a good lesson so that he can brag no more again in front of me."

"To be truthful," Jin told him, "my Dad has two concubines. One came from a whorehouse in the south and the other fled from her marriage. They often chattered with my aunties and sisters-in-law, showing off their savvy as married women. I was quite aware of what they talked about. Only I have been afraid of being too violent, which might do harm to your health. But I can be very wild. Put any very hard cock in my cunt and have a try. It doesn't matter if it's built of well-tempered iron, windmill-ground bronze, antelope's horn or diamond, it'll wear itself out in there all the same."

"We'll see, dear," said Easterngate. "Now allow me to come to a halt, for you need a quick snooze before engaging in a battle with him later this evening."

He wiped his penis clean and then wiped out her oozed fluid for her. He rose to leave, while she went to the bed to sleep.

Our story proceeds to Dali, now at home with his mother, ecstatic in anticipation of the rendezvous in the evening. He wrote a note to Easterngate before nightfall:

> *Any change to the assigned meeting? The ancient says that having a thousand pieces of gold is not as good as to obtain Ji Bu's promise.[6] Sister-in-Law is such a beauty, she is more valuable than a thousand pieces of gold, while Elder Brother, in his reputation for sincerity, outshines even Ji Bu. I have buckled on my armour and taken up my sword, ready to charge into the pink gate. To keep you in-formed, I am delivering this letter of challenge first. Ha-ha!*

After reading it, Easterngate wrote a reply:

> *Derisible! Listen, Penetrator of Hairy Grotto! She says she wants me to tell you that she has gotten her battle array well deployed. If you do not have a powerful bow and sharp sword, she is afraid that you may not be able to dash into her bastion. Go get some tributed treasures by northern monks. They may perhaps help you a bit for the bout you are so eager to take. This is my reply.*

Having read through the letter, Dali looked up and found that the sun had set and a bright moon was rising. He set out for Easterngate's study.

"You are early!" said Easterngate with a smile. "Too impatient, aren't you?"

Dali grimaced. "Elder Brother, please be kind! The earlier I meet her, the more pleasure I can enjoy."

"Okay, just wait here," Easterngate bade him. "It'll take her a while before she can be out with you."

"No problem, I'll wait for her," Dali said.

Easterngate went into the bedroom. Jin had just awakened from her sleep and was about to rise. Easterngate threw his arms around her, bellowing, "Darling, you have been sleeping for a whole day!"

So saying, he reached down into her slit.

"Whoa," he blurted out in astonishment, "it's soaking wet!"

"You talked to me too much about sex," she replied, "and just now I dreamed that somebody was making it with me. That's why."

"Who was the guy screwing you in your dream?" Easterngate queried.

"That's none of your business," Jin smirked.

She slid her hand onto his hard-on and grabbed it.

"Darling, fuck me hard until I'm satisfied!"

"My prick is not quite up to it," said Easterngate. "To have some really satisfying enjoyment, you need Dali's large cock, which can thrust into your deepest recesses. He is now in the study waiting for you. Come on, let's go see him!"

Jin let loose a cackle.

"I was just joking with you!" she said. "I didn't mean I would really get into it."

"Damn it," Easterngate gruntled. "There are always those women who tend to whitewash themselves before their husbands, but behind their backs, they'll stop at nothing to keep a lover. You should not follow in their footsteps!"

"Sweetheart," Jin laughed, giving him a hug, "I admit I have long been considering an affair. But I'm very afraid of you. If you don't blame me, I would certainly like to make love with him. Remember you once asked me to keep him company in drinking? His good looks and well-built body drove me wild! The day before yesterday it was sweltering and he wore no pants. I saw his hard boner throbbing under the thin material of his vest, making a tent of the part that covered it. My fluid flowed out so copiously that it thoroughly soaked my silver-red drawers! There are still some recognizable traces on them. Go take a look if you want. Now you are urging me to see him. All right, I'll just do as you ask. I'm so in love with you that I have told you everything in my mind, even the innermost secrets. You should never sneer at me in your heart!"

"This is what I want you to do," said Easterngate, "so you needn't worry that I'll blame you or despise you. Just come with me. He has been waiting outside for a long time."

"Wait, wait," Jin cried, "I haven't bathed my feet yet!"

"You are really a sound sleeper!" Easterngate laughed. "You even forgot having had a wash, and now, at this moment, are going to make last-minute preparations! Anyway it's important. Let me help you bathe."

He fondled her pussy while cleaning it for her.[7]

"Such a charming thing is now going to become tasty meat for him!" he sighed. "Listen, do it just once and then come back to our room immediately, okay?"

"Whether or not I can go to him, you have the final say," Jin returned. "But now that you have given me permission, it'll be none of your concern any more even if I do it twice!"

She stood up, drying her privates and asking him to pass her a pair of drawers.

"Well, well," said Easterngate, "you'd better go without them, for you'll soon strip them off anyway."

"Don't talk nonsense," Jin chided him. "Women like men to pull at their underpants; that's the most exciting moment for them. Understand?"

She put on her drawers and dressed herself up.

Easterngate caressed her bound feet.

"What a nice pair of small feet!" he said. "You should change into your red shoes, and then, as Dali sets your legs over his shoulders, which he sure will do I believe, he'll be thrilled."

Jin changed into her red shoes. Before going, she bade Easterngate to fetch some towels for her from underneath their bed mat. Easterngate handed her the towels.

"Now you have been fully armed!" he remarked.

Hand in hand, they walked to the study.

Jin came to a stop at the doorway, saying, "I am feeling uncomfortable. It's really too embarrassing for me!"

"You see him everyday," Easterngate cheered her on, "and when you are alone with him, you'll feel all right."

He pushed her forward, calling Dali to open the door.

"Look, you are going to have a wonderful night!" he pronounced bitterly. "It has taken me every ounce of strength to get her here!" After pushing her into the room, he locked them in and shouted, "I'm leaving!"

Upon hearing this Jin deliberately turned around, pretending to rush out.

Dali seized her firmly. "Darling, there is no escape," he cooed, planting a kiss on her mouth. "You must let me do it today!"

Easterngate was peeping from outside a window.

Now Dali was carrying Jin to a bench with a lamp nearby. He set her on it, and with his eyes riveted on her face, muttered, "Dear heart, you are indeed a vision of beauty!"

He gave her six or seven kisses, his hand reaching down for her crotch. Jin tightly held her skirt, withstanding his intrusion.

"Wait a moment," she said, leaning over to blow the light out.

Dali stopped her. "Leave it on, to shed some light on your charms," he said.

He pulled, with all his might, at her drawers. The band came loose. He rolled them down and finally put his hand on her nether regions.

"Oh my dear," he groaned, pinching her pubic skin gently, "it's fantastic!"

He dragged her to the bed and wasted no time in getting her skirt and drawers off. Then he parted her thighs, ready to plunge himelf into her crevice. Jin played coy and shy, covering her face with her sleeve.

Dali pulled it away.

"Darling," he said, "we see each other every day and are quite familiar. You needn't feel so ashamed." He then peeled off her remaining garments.

Jin was now naked. Her skin was so white that lying on her back in bed she looked as lovely as a white jade sculpture. Fondly, Dali held her face with both his hands, gazing at her in admiration.

"Darling," he murmured, "I see you every day and you don't know how many times you got my prick stiff! Tonight I have finally had this opportunity to live my fantasies out!"

Jin was turned on and started to squirm. With one good shove Dali pushed his shaft deep into her, which she engulfed without much difficulty. He then moved in and out ceaselessly, and in not more than a hundred strokes, wonderful tingles of pleasure began racing all over him. His sperm could not help spilling out, abundantly.

"You are so quick!" Jin scoffed.

"Don't laugh, please," Dali grinned. "It became hard around noon, and remained standing all the time I was waiting for you. Too impetuous. That's why once you were in front of me, with all your charms and grace, I was unable to hold back. This is our first encounter and you must allow me to flaunt some of my skills!"

Jin rose to leave, putting on her clothes.

"Wait," he called, "where are you going in the middle of the night? I haven't started yet!"

As he had come, he could not harden his limp organ right away. Fearful that she might see through him, he struggled to prop himself up and carried her back to the bench by the window.

"Let's do it here," Dali said. "I'd like you to be lit by the lamp. Tonight I won't let you go until I tire out."

He laid her down on the bench and bent forward over her, looking her up and down closely. After giving her six or seven kisses intermingled with some slurping suckings of her tongue, he said, "Darling, although I see you every day and am quite familiar with your face, I haven't so far taken a good look at your body and pussy. I must take advantage of this opportunity to get an eyeful!"

He began by twiddling her breasts, which were smooth and round, lying flat on her chest. Her skin felt fine, and stroking it with his hand, he found there was not a single crease on it, which married women having given birth to children would usually have. As he moved downward to her waist, he could not help bursting out, "What a slender waist!" He let himself move on, across her belly, and down further onto the mound, which protruding, resembled a steamed bun in contour, with only sparse soft pubic hair on it. He kneaded and tweaked it in a variety of ways, and then opened her thighs, prying into it. It looked like an overripe red peach split open in the middle.

Jin hooked her feet around his head and pulled it toward her. Dali needed no further prompting and settled on the length of her slice at once. He licked and smacked, and then stuck his tongue into the hollow and vigorously lapped around in it. Jin was overwhelmed with a wild glorious sensation, her labia opened, shivering in spasms, and a burst of hot fluid came streaming out of the crack. Dali's penis grew rigid again. He clasped her hips, tugged them to the edge of the bench and lifted her feet high against his shoulders.

"Honey," he groaned, focusing his gaze on her small feet, "they are really a pair of three-inch golden lotuses!"

"The other day," he continued, holding her feet in his hands, "I felt so happy to touch your foot as I pretended to pick up my chopsticks on the floor. I never expected that tonight I would be able to peel off your leggings and fondle your feet as much as I like!"

With this he drove in to the hilt, sending a jolt of delight all over her body.

Jin shrieked, "You are butting against the heart of my cunt! What a pleasure, even when you don't move!"

Dali began riding her furiously, and did not pause to catch his breath until he had given her about two hundred strokes. Jin tingled all over.

"You are driving me crazy, my dearest dearest sweetheart!" she screamed and embraced him. "I'm now no longer feeling ashamed. I can't take it any more! I'll use the techniques I learned as a girl to hump you wildly. Please don't laugh at me!"

She raised her hips and pressed them against his groin before starting her ramming. Her eyes closed and her head tilted to one side, she wiggled her legs and rocked her bottom with great force, moaning and crying in all kinds of voluptuous ways. Her vagina opened and contracted alternatively, grinding against his penis as it slid in and out. When he thrust hard, she clamped hard, and when he slowed down, she eased up. Finally, a gush of her hot torrent blasted forth, soaking his erection thoroughly and making his pumping emanate a ceaseless crackling noise.

Easterngate had been watching outside the window for some time. He was highly aroused. Hot and bothered, he grabbed his own rising member and began rubbing it. He rubbed it while watching them in action, until jolts of sperm jerked off, splashing on the wall beneath the window.

She is my beautiful wife, he thought. It is painful to see her stripped naked and fucked by him over and over again with her thighs so wide apart. I suckered myself into believing that he could save my johnson a hard job. Who would have expected that she would give herself to him in pure lust, servicing him with such great pleasure! This is an utterly unprofitable exploit for me!

He was angry. Yet as he was so in love with his wife and thought that he himself had sent her out to him, he decided to leave them alone. Sullenly he trudged back to the bedroom.

The maid Saihong was dozing as he entered. She leaned against a small table with a picture scroll hanging above it.

She has been very afraid of her fierce matron, thought Easterngate. Every time I slept with her, she shuddered with fear. I should start with some reminiscences of our flirtations, to make her feel at ease.

He tiptoed toward her and kissed her on the mouth, his arms wrapping around her. Seeing her remain still, he thrust out his tongue, and with its tip, pried twice at her teeth.

Saihong was awakened from her dream.

"Eeyuch," she cried. "Who is this?"

"It's me," he replied, with a big smile. "Who did you think it was?"

"It's very late now," Saihong said. "Why don't you go to bed? I beg you not to bother me like this at this hour!"

Easterngate whispered in her ear, "Your matron is not here and we can have some steamy pleasure!"

The maid hesitated. "Mother will be back soon, I am afraid."

"Your mother is now in the middle of fucking in that room," Easterngate told her. "She has dumped me to sleep with another guy, so we have every reason to score ourselves!"

"You are so kind to me," said Saihong. "It's just that I'm not quite capable and may botch things up."

They went to Jin's bed. Easterngate undressed and lay down beside her. Lying on her back, Saihong quickly wiggled out of her skirt and drawers and let her master poke his way inside. Spent because of his masturbation, Easterngate was rather impotent. One thrust and his penis lost its erection, shrinking and dwindling like a slug withdrawing its head.

Saihong laughed. "Your cock is screwing itself!" she said.

Her comment made Easterngate feel rather embarrassed. Seized by a sense of shamefulness, he grabbed his prick with haste and tried to yank it back into shape. Unfortunately, he only saw the last dribbles of sperm squeeze out of its peehole. It grew even softer, like a gob of flaccid cotton.

"What a trashy thing!" said Saihong. "It's good for nothing but getting me a bad name. I'll sleep with Axiu, and you can take care of yourself!"

"It won't be any big deal," Easterngate sputtered, "if you sleep here without having intercourse. Maybe a little later I'll be hard again. You'd better stay until I make you satisfied."

"I would rather not sleep with you," she said. "Do you think there is fun for a palace girl sleeping with a eunuch? She can only arouse herself by feeling and touching, but will never be able to fulfill her desire!"

Easterngate gave up. If I insist that she sleep with me, he mused, I probably can't sustain myself. He then released his reluctant companion, letting her get out of bed. In the meantime, he turned on his side to sleep.

Our story goes that Dali was thrusting into Jin on the bench. He thrust into her a thousand times or so, until she was dripping wet.

"Are you feeling good, darling?" he asked

"Nothing can make me feel better," Jin answered. "Thrills are now tingling down to the marrow of my bones."

Dali withdrew himself and then, burying his head between her legs, ate her pussy again. When he took a close look at it, he found there was a black mole on it.

"I'll definitely pass the examination!" he declared, giggling.

Jin was curious.

"What has made you say that?"

"According to what I have heard from a physionomist, a woman who has a mole on her genitals is bound to be granted the title 'Lady.' Since you are to become an official's wife, I'll no doubt be an official!"

"Don't talk nonsense!" said Jin. "Get up and thrust into me good!"

Once again Dali entered her, and thrust with all the vigour he could muster, but pounded lightly, moving in and out in a fast tempo. After eight hundred strokes, he shoved the entire length of his shaft into her snatch till it reached its heart, and then rammed against it in grinding gyrations. Not more than a dozen scrapings and Jin had passed out, her body becoming numb all over, motionless, and her mouth and tongue growing cold. Only with the air Dali blew into her mouth did he finally bring her back to consciousness.

"Oh, my dearest sweetheart, you have nearly stabbed me to death!" she cried and embraced him as she opened her eyes.

She then looked him in the eye affectionately, saying, "My dearest, sweetest honey, you should have become my husband! I'm sorry that Heaven didn't make me your wife."

"If you are not my wife," Dali teased, "then what do you think you are?"

"Your mother," she said.

Dali guffawed. "Aren't you saying that you are my 'little mother,'[8] the 'mother' with the word 'little' before it?"

"You can," Jin chuckled, "if you want, take me as your 'little mother.' Then I must charge you for your whoring tonight!"

Dali gave her a big hug. "Honey, should I be able to find as pretty and sexy a 'little mother' as you, I would not grudge paying her a hundred taels of silver for a night."

"Give me the money! Give me the money!" she demanded, laughing.

They poked fun at each other for a while.

"Well, enough of the joking," Jin said. "I'm now thinking of playing with you in a different way. I need your cooperation. You can pay me money for my service if you find it satisfactory."

"Tell me what it is," Dali said

"Let's go to the bed first!" she said.

Stark naked, they got into bed together, with their arms encircling each other's necks. Jin instructed him to lie on his back, and she herself straddled his body. She then turned herself around, and grabbing his manhood in her hands, sucked and licked it, flicking her tongue around its head periodically. Meanwhile, she positioned her opened vulva above his mouth and brushed against it, urging him to perform oral sex.

"This is what is called the 'reversed lovemaking position,'" she explained. "It can make even an iron man beg a truce. Have you ever tried it?"

"Oh, it's so good!" Dali gasped.

Then he responded to her question: "I've heard about it, but I myself have never done it before. Oh dear, I really can't stand it!"

Jin gripped the tip of his hardness in her mouth without releasing it for a mimute.

"I can't hold on any longer," Dali cried out. "I'm going to ejaculate. Don't blame me." His sperm exploded.

Jin gorged every spurt of cum he had emptied in her mouth.

"It feels wonderful, honey," he said. "Could you please turn around now?"

"Wait a minute. I want to suck your crank back to erection," Jin said.

She stroked it, sucked it. It grew crimson and swollen again. Then she turned around and sank down on his turgid phallus until she had it entirely encased in her clam. She bumped and squeezed rhythmically, her hips writhing fervently to the motions. Dali ejaculated again, unleashing a huge load, about the amount of a cup and half, inside her. He felt tired.

"What a rarity it is, darling!" he grunted, holding her tight on his belly. "My prick is very limp now and yet it can still hold it fast inside. It's indeed a lecherous cunt! Well then, lay yourself back on my body and sleep a while."

"No, I want it hard again!" said Jin.

"Have mercy," Dali implored. "I'm now too exhausted to get a hard-on. I'll come serve you tomorrow night, all right?"

"Is there another businessman like you," Jin mocked, "who wants to get a good deal next time?"

"In fact, I haven't enjoyed myself to the full," Dali told her. "I have some special feats you must see. Promise you'll come see me tomorrow?"

"To be honest with you, I haven't been satisfied either. I promise I'll see you tomorrow evening. I really don't know how you can beat me."

"Should you fail to show up," Dali threatened, smiling, "I'd die for you!"

"Trust me," she assured him. "I'll leave my drawers with you as a pledge and go back in wearing just this thin skirt."

"That would be great!" he exclaimed.

Roosters began crowing, and they saw through the window that a dim glow had emerged outside.

Jin said, "I have to go back in now."

She donned her outfit, bound her feet, and put on her shoes. When she was getting off the bed, she could not help fondling his organ once again.

"How come," she said, "you have been endowed with so big a wand, so long and rough a weapon like a saw? It has veins and ridges all over it and they were all protruding as it filled me, leaving virtually not a tiny bit of room for a whiff of air. That's really amazing! I have heard that there are good cunts and bad cunts. The good cunt has five strengths: it is tight, warm, fragrant, dry, and shallow, while the bad cunt has five failings: it is loose, cold, stinky, wet, and deep. Mine is tight and warm to be sure. As for the flavour, I have to ask my sweetheart. I know I'm not dry and shallow down there, but I'm pretty certain that no one can claim it's stinky."

"Dear heart," said Dali, "I am not quite sure if I could say that your pussy is on the tight side."

"Well," Jin retorted, "if mine is not slack enough, how was it able to accommodate your big dong so comfortably? Actually, the cock also has five strengths and five failings. Yours is not like those which are short, tiny, soft, supple or pointed. It is, on the contrary, large, hard, thick, forceful, and full of stamina. Such a good cock is hard to find. Easterngate comes quickly every time he couples with me, like a rooster playing in water. Moreover, he can never make it taut again once he has blown his wad. Yours is certainly beyond comparison. It's a live gem, indeed! Even a virtuous woman leading a happy married life can't resist its temptation. But now you have ejaculated and are no longer able to rise. I hate you! I must have more sucking on it until I feel I have gotten enough!"

She made his limp appendage stand at attention and kept mouthing and licking it for some time before taking her leave. Dali saw her to the door and gave her five kisses on the mouth, sucking so hard that she felt a burning sensation on the tip of her tongue. Meanwhile, he slid his hand down to her pussy, kneaded and caressed it, and then stuck his fingers into the furrow and insolently dug into its interior a few times. Jin, in return, seized his cock in hand, squatted down and gave it a bite.

"What fun if I could bite it off!" she said.

"Spare me, dear," Dali pleaded. "If you really want to, come see me earlier this evening."

"Okay, sure!" she said.

Then they parted from each other.

Jin returned to the bedroom. Seeing her husband had awakened, she embraced him and said, "My darling, I beg your pardon for having been away from you for the whole night."

"How did things go?" Easterngate asked.

"I won't tell you!" she said.

She scrambled to get astride him and tucked his bulge into her parted folds. It was, however, not hard enough yet to enter her until after she had ground on it awhile.

"Tell me everything you did with him," said Easterngate. "He did you the full night and you still want more from me? Haven't you been fully satisfied?"

Jin then told him the story in detail, from beginning to end.

"You should go laugh at him," she said, "telling him that he was a useless good-for-nothing, capable only of being a scrounger! But his cock, in all fairness, is stunning. No sooner it tunnelled into me than I felt tingles of pleasure running through my entire body."

With that she dove to hug him.

"Tonight, I'd like to sleep with him again," she said. "Do you agree, sweetheart?"

Easterngate laughed. "I can't lure you any more," he roared. "You are just like a little kid. Give you a candy and you want more. Honey, it's not that I'm objecting to your request; only I'm afraid you might be too tired."

Jin squirmed on top of him as he spoke. Unable to hold back his pent-up sperm, Easterngate shot off in her. Jin dislodged herself from him, and then fetched a towel, wiped off his cum, and cleaned herself up.

Now the sun was three feet high in the sky.

Easterngate said, "Dali must still be sleeping. I'll write a note to laugh at him."

He wanted to rise to write the note, but was seized by a fit of giddiness, obviously resulting from the intercourse. He then asked Saihong to bring him the inkslab he had encased in that purple sandalwood casket, and Axiu to fetch the Luo Longwen[9] ink stick packaged in an ancient carved box. As Axiu was grinding up the ink for him, Easterngate took out a pink-coloured "Licentiate School" letterhead, and leaning toward the edge of the bed, began to write:

> *My Younger Brother, you have been defeated three times by the Jin.[10] It seems that no one in the Southern Song army was strong enough. Where has your zest to conquer Cui gone?[11] How come you could only beg to surrender, crestfallen?! Even Emperors Huizong and Qinzong[12] did not suffer a worse humiliation than you did. Derisible!*
>
> *Younger Brother, you should raise your troops and launch a comeback right away, to restore our dignity. You must not allow the Nuzhen to enjoy success and feel superior to our Southern Song court, thinking that we don't even have one single matchable combatant!*

Having finished the writing, he called his page-boy Yutao to send the letter to the junior mister in the study. Yutao had been serving his apprenticeship as a singer at the Old Hanging Screen Alley in Beijing when Easterngate first met him. Attracted by his good looks, Easterngate bought him and made him his new partner for anal pleasures.

Yutao took the letter and went to the study. Dali was combing his hair as the boy came in to submit the letter to him. He burst out laughing as he read it, and wrote a reply at once:

> Yesterday I took the enemy lightly and that is how I lost Jieting.[13] I feigned defeat, with the purpose of letting my opponent feel complacent. But in your letter my submission is inappropriately overstated. Presenting a woman's headdress to me could not have made me more wrathful.[14] Tonight I shall go forth to battle again, fully armed, to see who will be the winner. I will furrow the enemy's court at least three times and tear open the bare recess where no man has ever reached! I will not stop until I destroy the lair and get rid of all the stench! This is my reply.

With this letter in reply Yutao went back to Easterngate, who tittered after reading it. He then read it out loud to Jin and asked, "Are you afraid?"

"No, not at all," she replied. "Tonight I'll make him drop to his knees and beg me for mercy! He said he wants to thrust me hard enough as to rip my cunt apart. And he also mentioned something of foul smell. Has he said anything else, anything that is not just detestable in his letter? I'll go see him tonight in any case, even without your permission! Please write him a reply for me, telling him that I'll cut off his monk head, skin his general, and snatch away his two eggs, and that I'll put them all in a vigourously boiling pot to cook until they turn into a mashed pudding altogether!"

"Well said!" Easterngate exclaimed. "There is no need to write it down. I'll just tell him what you said when I see him."

They called Saihong to bring their clothes, dressed, and got out of bed. It was already time for lunch.

Who would have thought that Dali had met a Buddhist quite adept quite in the art of the bedchamber who had given him two packages of sex pills. On one package were written these directions:

> *This aphrodisiac is for external application on men's jade stalk. It can make the organ larger, harder, and stand firm for a whole night. Caution: Without the application of an appropriate antidote, the user may not be able to release his semen up to ten days.*

On the other package the directions ran as follows:

> *This aphrodisiac is designed for insertion in a woman's orifice. It can make the cervix tight and dry, and the vulva lips hot and swollen. The sore and tingling sensation it produces in the interior will pleasure the user so much as to make her climax several times in succession, with her female*

fluid seeping out ceaselessly. Caution: Using more
than one pill without detoxification treatment will
cause the vagina much pain and swelling, which
can last for a number of days and look as awful
as an engorged male penis. To make the swelling
go down, spray a mouthful of cold water on the
infected parts and wash them in water with cured-
hay concocted in it.

There was an appendant warning on it as well:

This aphrodisiac should be applied to prostitutes
only. Good women should avoid using it, since it
may reduce their life span, and moreover, its over-
dosage may result in an irrecoverable debility.

Having read through the instructions, Dali smiled.

"I'm sorry I have no other choice," he muttered.
"Tonight I'll have to use them, to make her suffer in my
hands!"

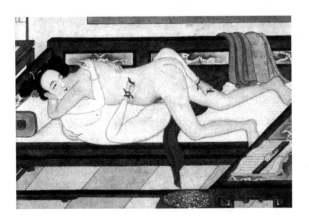

He first took a pill, which he applied on the head of his penis, and then took another one and tucked it into the knot of a towel. He had an ivory dildo which was made by a well-known Hui[15] artisan in Yangzhou. He put it inside his sleeve.[16] Now he looked forward to a fine evening.

Let's now turn to Easterngate who had finished his lunch. He was about to take a nap when a messenger from the school came to see him, announcing, "The Commissioner for Education will be stopping by our region en route to Huai-an tomorrow, and it is requested that students go meet him in Guazhou."[17]

Easterngate hurriedly called Yutao to bring him his coat and cap. He said to Jin before taking his leave, "I'll have to stay out tonight. When he comes, you can let him sleep in our bedroom and that'll make things a lot easier for you!"

"I won't do such things when you are away," Jin said.

"You can do anything you like as long as you don't block me out of your mind," Easterngate replied. "I'm going now. I'll tell him how you hate him, and will ask him to come see you earlier this evening. I won't be back until tomorrow. But don't take it for granted that he has great skills or something. I'll see if you remain unhurt."

Jin nodded, smiling, and saw him to the door.

Back in the room, she could not help feeling overjoyed. "What a miraculous fluke that was!" she chanted. "With such a good opportunity tonight, we can abandon ourselves without reserve."

She made the bed again, specially. Feeling quite aroused, she closed the door, eased down her drawers and lounged back on the tippler's recliner. Her legs lifted up and her pussy wide open, she looked at herself in the mirror.

"It's indeed good-looking," she said to herself, ramming

her fingers into the wet creases. "It looks attractive even to myself, not to mention how my new sweetheart loves it."

Seeing the two labes throbbing faintly, she smiled.

"You two pieces aren't making a good show! Yesterday you just got your rumpy-pumpy for a whole night and how could you have become so hungry again? Haven't you had enough?"

She then proceeded to look at her hindquarters.

"Men love rectal reamings," she murmured. "Tonight he'll do that to me for sure. I must take care not to let him get filthy stuff out as he has anal sex with me. I once heard Yutao say that squeezing some laver in the bung may help clean the internal muck."

She washed her lower part thoroughly in jasmin water.

"How could he know," she sighed, "that I'm making such preparations for him, for servicing him and making him happy!"

As she dried herself, she cried, "My new sweetheart, why don't you come right now? Why do you want to wait until evening? I'm impatient as hell and can't wait a second!"

Our story goes that Easterngate went through the hall to the study where his Younger Brother was staying. Dali, however, was gone already. The news had also reached him about the visit of the Commissioner for Education and he was inquiring if he should go see him when he bumped into the messenger from the school. He gave the messenger several maces of silver and therefore obtained an exemption from making the trip.

Easterngate strode out into the street and before long came across Dali. "The Commissioner for Education is coming to our school," he told him. "All the students on the list must go see him, so I can't return home tonight. Are you going as well?"

"I met the messenger just now and he said I don't have to," Dali replied.

He then told him how he had gotten permission.

"Since you have been exempted," said Easterngate in a low voice, "you can come see her this evening. I have told her to get the bed ready for you. You know you really pissed her off!"

"No problem, no problem," Dali mumbled. Parting with Easterngate, he could not help being beside himself with joy.

He thought, since Eastergate is away, why do I have to wait until this evening? He then began to move toward their residence. The two maids both dozed off after lunch and silence reigned in the house. Dali went straight into the bedroom.

Hearing somebody coming in, Jin asked, "Who is this?"

"It's me," he answered.

Jin was pleasantly surprised. Putting on her skirt in a hurry, she rushed to the door and shouted, "How dare you come straight in to the bedroom!"

"Open the door!" Dali begged in a low tone. "I'm afraid somebody is around."

"I won't open the door for you unless you drop to your knees first," she said.

Dali had to kneel down on the ground. Jin opened the door and burst into giggling. She hastily helped him to his feet and then they entered the room together, closing the door behind them.

"My sweetheart," Jin said, wrapping her arms around him, "I just think of you and here you come!"

"I simply can't believe that we have got such a heaven-sent opportunity for pleasure!" Dali responded.

Looking around, he saw that on the east side of the room hung a Qiu Shizhou picture of beautiful women,[18] and they looked as if they were real.

"I might as well take it as your lovemaking portraiture," he quipped.

Beneath the picture there was a long, elaborately-made Laizhou side table on which numerous antiques and various kinds of ars erotica were diplayed. Against the bed stood a dresser and there an ivory-inlaid cosmetic casket, filled with legumes, cypress leaves and bits of *nanmu*, sent out a waft of fresh aroma. The headboard of the bed was crafted in mottled bamboo and featured a mosaic of the word *wan* [ten thousand]. Over the bed hung a bluish white mosquito net with the embroidery of hundreds of butterflies. A finely woven mat spread on the bed, and on the mat were a long rattan pillow and two thin quilts encased in flowery, double-reticulated silk covers. The bedding was highly scented with the perfume of agalloch, emitting a strong, stinging frangrance. Right beside the pillow was placed a little round box made in the Song dynasty. It had an oval-shaped golden interior and lacquered outward finish with peonies of twin buds painted on it. A real *mianling*, imported from Burma, lay inside it.

Easterngate was incapable of pumping for long and his quick sex often left Jin unfulfilled. That was why he needed this little thing to do some complementary work.

"Last year," said Dali, having glanced aroudn the room, "I went to Nanjing to take the Provincial Examination. One day I was with Ma Lanxiang[19] in the pleasure quarters. Her bed and its covers were very similar to yours. In spite of being a well-known courtesan, she is nonetheless disappointedly inferior, not even a match for a fine hair on the sole of your foot!"

So saying, he threw his arms around her and gave her a kiss on the mouth.

"Quick, honey," he pressed, "take off your clothes and let me put it in."

"Go shut the windows, please," Jin bade him. "It's too bright, making me feel it shameful to undress."

"What's shameful between us?" Dali said with jest. "The brighter the better!"

He closed only the lattice screen windows.

Jin let him strip her, until she hadn't a stitch of clothes left. Dali felt her pussy with his hand, saying, "It seems that I got it swollen last night. Could you please open up so that I can have a look?"

This was simply a camouflage. His real intention was to put his pill in without letting her know about it. Jin of course was unaware of his trick.

"I'm plump and that's why it may look swollen," she said, lying back down and spreading her thighs. "Dali," she called, "come take a look! You could never make it swollen unless you have an iron-made cock!"

Dali put the pill on his finger and sent it in, pretending that he was frigging her.

"Indeed, it's not swollen yet," he said, grinning. "But I'll make it swollen later on!"

Jin laughed. "Should you have been so potent, I would be willing to let you do it any way you want. Be a true man! I wouldn't beg you for mercy even if I couldn't stand you."

"All right. Just remember what you said!"

Jin jumped up.

"I have been stripped naked," she railed, "but you keep talking away with your clothes on, still well-dressed!"

She removed his clothes and pulled down his pants. His

huge python jutted out before her eyes. She grasped it at once with both her hands.

"Darling," she said, "you seem to have feasted on eels today. Otherwise how could it become larger than last night?"

"Are you afraid?" Dali teased.

"There is hardly a cunt in the world that can't take in a cock," she teased back. "Only the cock may find itself too small in there. I just want it big to enjoy some good action, so how can I be afraid of it? As the saying goes, 'An opened mutton restaurant is ready to serve even the biggest tummy in the world!'"

With this she began sucking and nibbling on his steeple.

"Sweetie," she went on, "the tip is the most lovely part of the whole thing, you know? No skin on it, only the veins and ridges standing out and pulsating, it gave me great shivers of excitement as it brushed against my vulva."

By this time the inserted pill was beginning to take effect. Jin felt her vagina hot and sore, with so ichy a titillation that she could hardly bear it. She had to get up, and moved to the tippler's recliner. Her legs spread and her hands holding the arms of the chair, she spoke to Dali, "Why am I feeling so hot inside? So sore and itchy?"

"Well, I guess you are very horny," he replied. "What else do you think can account for this?"

"But usually I don't feel like this," Jin disagreed. "The feeling is very different, not like those I had before."

"Well, you have that sort of sensation only when your female fluid is about to come."

Jin groaned. "Quick, sweetheart! I need your thrust badly."

Dali was purposefully tardy. He only lightly nuzzled his dick against her outer furrows.

"I really can't stand it!" Jin shrieked.

Her body twisted, she wallowed her hips and rocked her legs and arms, looking as if she were greatly suffering with the spasms. Dali was stoked to see her wriggling in such a state. He laughed.

"I'm coming in now," he declared.

He plunged deep inside her and prodded hard for seven or eight hundred times without rest. Jin closed her eyes and drowsed off, her secretion seeping out at an alarming rate.

Women's essence, unlike men's semen, is light red and not very thick. At first hers looked like the spray of a sneeze, then it turned into something like a clear nasal mucus, and in the end it became a flow similar to a spurting spring. Dali crouched down and ate her creamy chum into his mouth. Very musky and sweet, the quantity was twice as much as a man's jism.

"What strange stuff," he said, smiling. "Now I finally know what women's juice looks like." He kept licking with his tongue until there was none of the residue left.

Jin opened her eyes. She had sobered up.

"Today I feel I'm very different," she said. "My cunt had an itch and I could hardly bear it. It was not like the feeling I had experienced before. It was so intense I felt as if there were thousands and thousands of caterpillars with pointed nibs biting me greedily inside. The tingles drilled into my bones, triggering jolts of burning and sore sensations. The harder you thrust into me, the more I suffered. Now I have been spent and feel slightly better."

She looked down at the floor.

"Plenty of fluids flowed out and why are they nowhere to be seen?" she asked.

"I have eaten them all," Dali told her. "Didn't you know that?"

Her soul had left her, so how could she have known about it?

But Dali had hardly finished his words when she burst out screaming, "Oh man! I feel I'm coming again! I'm spasming the way I did a moment ago."

She grabbed his prick in a hurry, and Dali made haste to let her guide it inside. Then, with full force, he started to hump her.

"I must make you feel good!" he swore after a thousand strokes.

Jin let out low, soft groans.

"Faster, and don't stop, sweetheart!" she begged. "Oh, I feel as if I'm dying and going to heaven. I can bear this no more!"

She fainted once again, her eyes shut, her mouth open, and her opened vulva flooding lavishly with a torrent of fluid. Dali again swallowed it into his mouth. He noticed that this time there was a more copious amount than her previous discharge.

Jin came around. "Funny," she said. "There was so much pleasure down there I felt as if I had been carried away into a state of celestial happiness. Should someone have put a knife to my head, I would rather have been killed than given up enjoying such an ecstacy. Now I have come around and see it is still the same cunt as before, so I just don't understand why you could cause so strong a surge of jollies, making me break out in a cold sweat. My mouth, my tongue, and my feet are all cold now. If Easterngate were here and saw all the mess on the floor, he would surely feel a pang. I must do the same to you, getting you to come in my mouth before letting you go!"

"Darling," Dali protested, "I have tried hard to cater to you, in the hope of making you happy. But you have rewarded me with this tirade. Take a good look at my iron cudgel. Where else could it be put but in your slimy cunt? Today I must fuck you well, fuck you to the exclusivity of your satisfaction!"

"You are setting me tingling again," Jin moaned.

In haste Dali plugged his prong back into her aperture. He first busted it seven or eight hundred times, then ground it a hundred times or so, and then pried at it another hundred times.

"This time," said Jin, "I won't allow you to eat my cum. Get a cup to hold it, so that I can take a look at it myself."

"Fine," Dali said.

He pressed vigorously against her pelvis, rubbing and ramming at her pubes for a while. Then he moved downward to her anus, where he nuzzled, scratched, and jimmied for some time before finally letting himself sink deep into her vagina.

Jin groaned, after two hundred thrusts. "I'm dying, sweetheart. I can't hold out any more. How can you make me go into such a frenzy of delight?"

Seeing her become semi-conscious, Dali withdrew himself. He sheathed his dick with the dildo he had brought along and then put it back in again. With might and main he pumped her five hundred times until she completely passed out. In a hurry he fetched a cup and placed it before her pussy. Jin came furiously this time, her hole wide open, the two labes fluttering and gasping like a split muzzle of a horse, and hot fluids erupting abundantly in orgasmic fervor, filling nearly half the cup. Dali noticed that this time she was discharging much more than she had in the first two sessions. He put the cup away by the side of the bed.

Jin woke up. She saw her own essence in the container. "That's funny," she said.

She asked him to drink it. Taking the cup from her hand, Dali smelled a strong, musky odor. He drank it up.

"Sweetheart, you are really a funny kink!" she blurted.

Then she said, "Since I have come three times already and you are also quite soft, I think I should go to the kitchen now to cook something to eat."

She rose and dressed, and then went to the kitchen to cook.

How sensible she is! And how lucky I am to have made love with such a woman! Dali mused, giving himself a good handjob briefly.

Our story goes that Jin was now going to the kitchen. By this time her pussy lips had become very swollen and she could not walk without feeling that something was in the way.

Look what has been done! she sneered at herself secretly. When he comes back home tomorrow and sees this, he'll laugh at me for sure.

"Saihong," she called her maid, "Mr. Zhao is now in my room and we are going to eat dinner inside today. Change into your clean clothes. You and Axiu should both wait upon us."

"Axiu," she then spoke to the other maid, "take a lamp into the bedroom!"

Axiu, taking a lamp with her, went into the bedroom. Dali pulled her to him and gave her a kiss on the mouth.

"Where is your mother?" he asked.

"In the kitchen," Axiu answered.

Dali held her tight.

"Can I make love with you for a while?"

"Oh no, Mother would beat me!" she refused, and then rushed out in a huff.

"Today," she said to Saihong, "Mother shut herself in the bedroom for a whole day. Do you know why? Because that guy was in there too. To think Mother is such a beautiful woman and has been ravished by him!"

"Mr. Zhao is a handsome young man," Saihong said, "and I think it was lucky for Mother to sleep with him!"

Now Jin had food prepared. She put it in a large compartmented tray. When she opened a jug of Three Whites wine, everything was ready for serving. She bade Saihong to carry the tray and Axiu the jug, and the three of them went into the bedchamber together.

Dali gave Jin a hug and said, "Thank you so much for preparing the dinner, honey!"

They set a small table at the foot of the bed. Dali took the seat of honour and Jin sat opposite him, with Saihong serving them the wine. They drank ten more cups each to begin with.

"I can drink no more just sitting here alone!" said Dali.

He moved over to the other side, right beside Jin, and pressed her to his bosom, with one hand holding the cup and the other feeling her pussy.

"Darling, why is it so swollen?" he asked. "Does it hurt?"

"Don't be so snoopy," Jin returned, smiling. "Just mind your own drinking."

She went on sipping. This time, without swallowing the wine, she transfered it to his mouth instead. She kept on sending him the drink this way until she drained four or five cups.

"Honey," Dali proposed, "I'd like to set the cup in your love mound. It would be fun to see the beverage spray out of it."

"Go ahead," she said. "It's not difficult, is it?"

She called Saihong to fetch a large glass, and after taking off her housedress, lay down naked on the lounge chair. Axiu and Saihong, as they had been instructed, raised her legs, cushioned her butt with a pillow and put the glass right into her gash. Dali imbibed four or five glasses.

"What fun!" he exclaimed. "What an excellent saucer it is!"

Jin moaned, "Oh dear, you have set my insides tingling again, like they did during the day."

"This is exactly what I was expecting," said Dali. "I want to concoct your juice with the alcohol!"

Jin grinned. "Fantastic idea, eh? Take the glass away and put your cock in quick. It's a pleasure to make love with me while quaffing."

"You bet!" said Dali. "For every hundred thrusts I'll drink a cup of wine."

"Sounds very good," Jin said.

She then turned to Axiu. "You count," she bade her. When you have counted a hundred times, ask Saihong to pour him wine."

Dali began thrusting, and after a hundred strokes, guzzled one cup.

"My cunt is very itchy," Jin moaned. "Fuck me faster and harder, please!"

At her entreaty Dali went all out to thrust, too fast for Axiu to count.

"I have thrust into you more than two hundred times!" he made an announcement himself, giggling.

"Then you can have two cups," Jin told him.

"Now I'll count myself," Dali said to Axiu. "I'd like to see how many times I must thrust to get your Mother come." He buried himself entirely inside her before proceeding to thrust, and he thrust her two solid hours.

Dali griped, "I have had no patience for this endless counting. Just pour me wine, as many cups as you like." He emptied ten more cups in succession, without a break.

"You have given me a thousand or more thrusts," Jin said, "but why have you only made me feel sore and itchy inside without getting my female essence out? Could you hump me even harder?"

With a vengeance, Dali pounded her, bucked her, for another several hundred times.

"I can't bear it any more!" Jin screamed. "I'm done for."

She fell into a swoon again, her face turned pallid, her hands and feet cold, her lips parted and her eyes closed. Dali, with haste, drew himself back and put the glass in front of her vulva immediately. Out her female essence flowed, as it had before, filling half the cup.

Saihong and Axiu both chuckled.

"What is this stuff?" they asked.

"Hot sap I drew forth from inside your matron," Dali replied. "Afterwards I'll do the same to you, too, until I get your juices to sluice out."

Seeing her mistress remain unconscious, Saihong was rather worried.

"What is happening to her?"

Dali growled, "This wanton adultress? She has burnt out! What do I keep her alive for?" His mouth, however, moved to press against Jin's as he spoke. After breathing some air into it, he saw her gradually open her eyes, and her hands, too, began to move about. Yet it took her a fairly long moment to come to her senses. She was bathed, completely, in a cold sweat.

"Well!" she was at last able to get herself vocal. "I enjoyed much more pleasure this time than during the day. I reached a climax, extremely rapturous. Only it has left my hands and feet very weak, though. Could you please lend me a hand so that I can sit up?"

Dali took her into his arms and made her sit on his lap.

"How is it that there is so colossal a load of cum in it?" she said, seeing her own emission in the glass.

She then turned to Saihong and asked, "Is it mixed with wine? Pour it into a small gold cup so that I can see exactly how much it is."

Saihong filled a small gold cup to the brim. The liquid, with the reflection of golden colour, looked clearer and more lovely. Dali took the cup from her hand and drained it at one gulp.

"Even nectar and sweet dew can't be more tasty than this," he said.

He then drank another three cups Saihong had poured him until there was none left.

"Amusing!" Jin remarked. "The ancient said aptly, 'Mouth sucking, waist clasping, and pussy squeezing, no matter how hard your cock is trying to resist ejaculating, I'll get its brains out, stickily soaking.' Now, I'll suck your tongue like mad to arouse your lust, clasp your waist tightly as to trigger your splash, and lock your dick hard enough to make you shiver all over. Although your globby knob is flushing thick and full, I haven't seen a single seed spill out. That's weird. I want you to come! And I want to eat your cum!"

Dali was amused. "You can, if you are able to get it."

"Incredible!" Jin sighed, grasping his rod in her hands. "It seems to have been well tempered."

She sucked and nibbled it alternatively; still nothing came out. She called Saihong and Axiu, "You girls come over here! I want you both to suck it, suck it until he spends, all right?"

Both of them looked rather reluctant

Jin flew into a rage.

"You slaves!" she cursed. "Don't look so unwilling. Haven't you seen that I sucked it? What do I want you for, uh?"

Saihong said to Axiu, "We have never been allowed to take a single look at Master's object, but now we are being forced to eat his as if it were our meal!"

Taking turns they sucked and licked. Saihong sucked until her gums grew weary; Axiu licked hard and her saliva went dry. Dali, however, remained rock hard as before.

"Strange," Jin said. "Stop, then."

She said to Dali, "I like watching people in action. Could you ride Saihong so that I can look on?"

"But my prick must be too large for this virgin," he replied. "I probably can't work her up quick enough for your satisfaction."

Jin laughed. "This sly fox has already made it with my husband," she told him. "The other day I went back to my parents' for a birthday get-together and she made it with him half a night. I gave her a good beating when I got home. Yesterday, I was told, she made it with him again for the whole night while I was in the study with you. Her hole must have been screwed big. Come on, strip your clothes off and let Mr. Zhao give you a thrust!"

Saihong felt so abashed that she turned away, refusing to come over.

"Isn't this your mistress?" Dali burst in. "Aren't you afraid of her?"

With a good shove he pushed her down onto the lounge chair. Jin helped him strip her and they finally undid all her clothes. Having witnessed a series of racy scenes during the day, Saihong had actually been very wet down there, her oozed secretion having made her underwear quite damp. Jin noticed this as it was being ripped off.

"Look," she said, tittering, "this slave girl seems to have pissed in her drawers."

"Really!" Dali said with a jest. "You are not saying that your cum in the glass is also urine?"

Saihong covered her mouth with her hands, snickering, She let him cleave her puffy labes with his thick cudgel, without protest, nor painful moans.

"It's impossible," Dali said, "that Master Easterngate could in two nights make your hole so big, unless he did it hundreds and hundreds of times a night."

"I did sleep with him several times," Saihong confessed. "That's why it is fairly loose. Please don't talk about it any more."

Jin roared with laughter upon hearing this. "This slave girl has the audacity to be bossy to you!" she said.

"Sir, give her a good screw!" Axiu egged on. "It's just that her pussy is too cheap to serve you. Better to sleep with Mother."

"This is her piece of luck and you shouldn't feel jealous," Dali said.

He then drove half way into her sphincter.

"Oh, you are bucking me too much," Saihong yelped. "I beg you to pull it out a little bit, please!"

Dali comforted her: "Calm down! I guarantee you'll enjoy pleasures soon."

After nearly four hundred strokes, Saihong began moaning, with barrages of mumblings *"aiya!" "aiya!"* emitting from her mouth from time to time.

Dali muttered, "I'll keep on working her until she comes!"

He braced himself up and pushed it in to the scrotum. After two hundred pumps, Saihong grew entranced, as Jin had before.

"Look," Jin was excited, "this slave girl is getting mesmerized."

"Yeah," said Dali. "Her teeth are clenched and her legs have given out, I can tell that she is about to spend."

Without delay, Jin put a glass before the jut of her pelvis. Soon her labia opened, panting, and fluids spewed forth in no time. In comparison with the cum of her mistress, hers was much less, only about the amount of one tiny cup.

Jin quipped, "It's quite stimulating to see this maid going into an orgasmic climax."

"Honey, watching you coming was even more intriguing," Dali told her. "The gate of your vagina is twice as big as hers, looking like the muzzle of a horse agape."

Yet in his mind he thought: Female essence comes less on its own and more when the aphrodisiac is applied, which no doubt will injure health.

Jin held the cup of Saihong's essence in hand and urged Dali to drink it.

If I drink it, he pondered, she'll definitely feel mortified.

He then took the cup from her hand and poured the fluid on the floor.

"Why did you pour it out?" she asked.

Dali put his arms around her, replying, "Sweetie, I love you. That's why it didn't bother me to gulp down your slop. But how can I drink hers? It's so dirty!"

"Oh darling, I didn't know you are so in love with me!" Jin exclaimed. "I'll let you do it with me any way you want and I'll not complain a single word even if you pound me to a nad-shattering unconsciousness."

"My prick can't soften and I feel pain," Dali groaned. "Could you help me make my testicles recede, honey? I want you to open your thighs to let me get off."

"To be honest with you," said Jin, "the deeper part of my flue is still quivering for your thrusts. Only the outer part hurts so much with the swelling that I probably can't bear your busting again. Please leave me alone for a moment. You can do it with Axiu instead."

Dali pouted. "I don't like this small maid. Only screwing my sweetie can make me feel happy."

"Thank you for your loving affection. Then just don't mind too much about my minor suffering. I'd remain perfectly happy even if you were to make me die in your hands."

By this time Saihong had come around. She got up naked and went off to one side, putting on her clothes and laughing at Axiu.

Axiu laughed back at her too.

"How you were burning with lust!" she sneered, pointing her finger at her. "No wonder you could enjoy so much pleasure!"

Jin interrupted, "These legs of mine feel like they are coming off my body and I can't raise them. I want you both to come and help me lift them up!"

Dali took a close look at her red-hot cunt. He found its lips had swollen and the skin of the inner walls had been badly frayed. In the depth of her vagina a chunk of flesh stood out, looking like the protruding crest of a rooster. The gullet, full of steamy heat, looked as if it were being simmered on fire. He felt very sorry for her.

"Darling," he said, apologizing, "it makes my heart ache to see you suffering so great an agony."

He then lapped her swelling with his tongue.

Jin groaned. "Be tender, please!"

After licking awhile, Dali thought: Do I really have to show pity on her before she cries out for mercy?

He lodged his cock back into her twat again, and mustering all his strength, humped her very hard. Jin endured the pain, letting him pound as vigorously as he could for about a hundred times.

"I have to beg your pardon, sweetheart," she entreated, wrapping her arms around him. "I can't stand the pain any more. Please let me off, I beg you!"

I have enjoyed enough pleasures in her cunt, Dali mused, but not yet in her asshole. Why not do some anal reamings, to experience a greater fun?

He then gave her a hug.

"Considering your suffering, honey," he said, "I have decided to spare you the punishment. But how can I get my standing dick to subside when it refuses to? I wonder if you could let me ride from behind as your cunt is no longer available?"

"No, this is out of the question!" Jin said. "You don't know how many times he got my bawling-out just because he wanted to touch it. Now I'm having this request again, from my sweetheart! You know your meat mallet is way too massive, which I probably can't take in there."

Dali persisted. "Do you know how many times I have been screwed by your husband? I remember the first time he worked on me I was only fourteen. I suffered pains at the beginning and he only spit into my hole to lube it up. He even did it with me the day before getting married to you, and I felt so aroused that my pre-cum spilled out. He ate half of it and spat the other half into my bung, making it very slippery and loose then."

"In that case," said Jin, "you should also slather mine with some spittle before you start."

"That's no problem," Dali agreed.

Like a nancy-boy, she bulged her bottom while leaning against the bed, letting him do his rim-job until he greased her exposed rear opening thoroughly.

"You are so in love with me," she sighed, "licking this poop box of mine that no one else is willing to touch!"

In slow tempo Dali jacked his shaft into her hole. This was the first time Jin had her anus penetrated and the anguish was beyond endurance. She gritted her teeth, her eyebrows knit closely.

"How horrible you look as you scrunch up your face!" said Dali. "Are you feeling all right?"

"Don't mind me," she replied. "Just keep on riding."

"Honey, it seems that you are suffering, not feeling happy?"

"As long as you are happy, I'm happy," she said. "Please don't be so concerned about me, even if you pump me split and inflict violent pain on my body."

Dali crammed three inches into it and there he lingered still.

"Why don't you thrust?"

"I'm afraid that may hurt you," he said.

"But my ass will bring you no pleasure if you don't move," Jin told him. "Do whatever you like and just don't pay much attention to me!"

She felt her pussy and bung with her hand. There was only a thin layer of partition in between and the jacking actions in the rear aperture could also produce some stimulation in the front orifice. As her vaginal fluids seeped out, she asked Dali to withdraw and lube his dick with the secretion. Dali did as he was told, thus making her rear canal become much more lubricious.

Dali started thrusting, with great speed.

"Oh, my understanding babe!" he cried, happily.

Yet since her anus was full of fat and grease, he could not drive in to the base. Not more than five hundred thrusts or so and a lumpy fat from the depth had already stuck to his glans, which he brought out finally. He called Jin to look back at it.

"What is this?" she asked.

"This is called grease," Dali replied, "the function of which is to make the hole slippery. Honey, your ass is fabulous. It not only excels a nancy-boy's but also is much tighter than your own vagina. Being engulfed in there is really a great pleasure!"

After a pause he asked her, "Have you seen the note I wrote to Easterngate yesterday?"

"Yes I did," she said.

"Do you understand some of its implied meanings?"

"What you wanted to say was nothing but fuck me hard to rip my pussy apart."

"Let me tell you what," Dali said. "You did understand that 'furrow the enemy's court' and 'destroy the lair' mean 'to rip up your cunt,' but you have missed the metaphor 'tear open the bare recess where no man has ever reached.' By this I allude to the sodomy of your asshole. That hole has no hair on it, so if it's not a 'bare' recess, what is it?"

"You damned wretch!" Jin cursed, laughing. "Today you haven't missed anything you said in your letter, have you? Well now, get yourself hard to milk your balls! It's about to daybreak."

"All right," he said, "if you don't complain that my cockhead will buck you too hard."

Dali then started thrusting, and after four or five hundred strokes, withdrew himself in a quick, jerky motion, which brought out her rectal tube by three or four inches.

"Look!" he hollered, "What have I brought out?"

Jin looked down at it.

"This is the end of my rectum," she said. "It came out because of your violent withdrawal. An ugly thing, isn't it? How should we deal with it?"

"Well," Dali joked, "wait until more comes out and I'll make a tail for you."

"Don't laugh!" Jin was a little vexed. "It doesn't look nice, and besides, I'm aching with it, feeling suffocated in there. Could you please jam it in for me?"

"Honey, I'm sorry to have caused you so much pain," he apologized. "This little tail is now getting cold and you can't draw it back on your own contraction. I'll see if I can do something for you."

He crouched down and licked it, and then let his tongue alternate between licking and bucking, trying to make it shrink back.

Jin sighed, "No one else is willing to lick so filthy a crapper. I'm really grateful for what you are doing for me. Even if I were to die for you now, I'd do so without any regrets!"

Dali took a close look into the hole and found that another lump, black in colour, had also been drawn out.

"What is that black stuff?" he asked.

"Laver," she said.

"That is what I used for anal pleasures," said Dali. "How did you know about this trick?"

"From Yutao, the new catamite in our home," she told him. "He used to be a singer in the capital, and he told me all this when I asked him about it. Oh, the fallout hurts so, I feel as if my bung were being split."

"I guess I have to quit now," Dali grumbled. "But my prick is still very hard and I don't see any sign that sperm will be coming forth. Could you allow me to work on Axiu for a while?"

"Fine," said Jin. "This little maid is indeed good-looking, but as you know, she is very young."

She then turned to Axiu and called, "Come over here, quick!"

Axiu was reluctant.

"Mr. Zhao's bulge is scary and it'll sure hurt me," she murmured. "I'd prefer not to do it with him."

"Sooner or later you'll be laid by Mr. Zhao," the mistress pressed. "So why not do it now, in front of me? I'd like to watch it."

Saihong was delighted. "You laughed at me just now and now it's your turn! Come on, take off your pants!"

"I did feel turned on," Axiu said, "as I watched Mother come together with him. But I'm afraid I myself am too small to be up to it."

"Get your pants off first," Jin snapped.

At her mistress's order, Saihong began to pull at Axiu's clothes and finally she was stripped, standing naked to one side. She attempted to run away, but the elder maid seized her firmly.

"Get her onto the lounge chair," Jin bade Saihong, "and I'll keep a tight grip on her head."

Saihong forced Axiu to open her legs, and then pressed them with both her hands. Axiu was unable to move. She whined, "You are treating me like you were slaughtering a pig!"

"Good!" Dali shouted. "Look what a nice small pussy I have got! It doesn't even have a single fuzz!"

He felt it with his hand and said, "Boy, I haven't even touched you yet, but something like piss has already moistened it! Well then, let your Mr. Zhao open your maidenhead for you!"

"She is very young," Jin counselled him. "Much better to put some spittle on it so that she'll suffer less."

"No spittle for the virgin," Dali declared. "A capable man applies nothing like that to open a maidenhead. Now that she is wet, I'd better enter her right away."

He tapped her pussy with his pole.

"Oh, it hurts!" Axiu squealed. "Slow down please! I beg you to be gentle!"

Saihong, with a violent stir, splayed her legs wide apart. Taking advantage of this opportunity, Dali forced a large part of his glans into her fissure, his thrust giving off an explosive sound.

"Help, I'm dying!" Axiu yowled, a fountain of fresh blood spouting forth.

"Mother, spare me please!" she went on whining. "He is cutting me and I feel something has cracked inside. Too painful to stand."

"Only the top part is big," Dali conned her, "and down below it gets small."

Axiu begged once again, "Don't drill deeper, please!"

But Dali responded by giving her another hard push. With a similar snap, he finally anchored the whole bulb of his penis inside her, sending the maid into a desperate frenzy. Tossing her head and thrashing her arms and legs, she whimpered, "I am dying! I can't bear the piercing pain any more."

Her blood gushed forth along his shaft, dripping without cease.

"Good job!" Jin laughed. "You are thrusting her very well."

"Sir, keep on driving until your cock is entirely buried," Saihong goaded on.

"You nasty slave!" Jin scolded her. "Your cunt has been screwed big so you could take it comfortably. But this is her first time. How could she bear so vehement a thrust? Enter another two inches and she'll have an awful suffering."

Axiu cried, "Master Zhao, Madam Jin, please have mercy! Give me another bucking and that'll be the death of me!"

Dali pulled himself out.

"I still feel pain inside even without it," said Axiu.

She had no expectation that Dali had deliberately withdrawn himself in order to plunge in again with full force, and this time, accompanied by another similar explosive sound, he sent half of his stiffening erection inside.

"I'm dead!" Axiu gave out a high-pitched keening, tossing and bumping wildly.

Saihong clutched her legs fast.

"I'm dead!" she continued howling. "I really can't stand this torture."

"I'll let you go soon," Dali said.

He began thrusting, and thrust her over three hundred times, each time trying to stick it in to the hilt. As he was driving in and out, Axiu implored him once again, "I'm in a very bad way. Please don't move!"

Her plea was ignored, though. Dali kept on thrusting forcefully for another hundred times or so, until her blood splashed out all over the floor. Axiu writhed with pain, tears in her eyes and her face an ashen sheet. She lost consciousness.

"Let her off, then," Jin said. "This slave girl doesn't have good luck. You have only been half way inside and she has passed out."

In haste Dali pulled out. Saihong helped Axiu sit up. It took her a moment to come to.

She groaned, "I'm suffering an awful pang!"

No sooner had she opened her eyes than she groused at Dali, "Sir, you were so cruel! If you had kept on bucking me, you would have broken my small intestine. I am now having so much pain in there I can hardly bear it!"

She vented her grievance to Saihong when seeing her blood all over the floor.

"Mr. Zhao has wrecked me and I'll be a useless person all my life."

"Go to sleep!" Jin said.

"You laughed at me," said Saihong, "but actually I enjoyed it. How could you wind up like this?"

Axiu scrambled up. She went wobbling away, slowly.

Dali wiped his cock clean and then washed Jin's face for her. After having had breakfast, he was ready to leave. Jin, however, was still reluctant to separate from him. She grabbed hold of his member and sucked it once again. Finally he was let go. Since she herself was tired and her pussy was swollen, she went to the bed to sleep.

Easterngate had seen the Commissioner for Education off and was now returning home. Passing by the study, he saw Dali sleeping on the tippler's recliner. He sneaked in, quite aroused, and after removing his pants, poked his prick into his Younger Brother's ass. The latter did not wake up until after he had been jacked for a while.

"Oh, sweetheart!" he called, and stuck out his tongue into Easterngate's mouth, trying to be as servile as he could. It took Easterngate only a short moment to unleash his sperm. After that, they chatted briefly and parted.

Easterngate went into the main hall.

"Honey, I'm home," he said to his wife, who was lying in bed. "Can we enjoy ourselves for a while?"

"No," Jin replied. "I had a very bad intercourse last night and ended up getting my pussy broken. You can't do it with me now."

Easterngate took off the covers and found that her vulva lips were turgid and the skin of the interior walls was broken.

"My goodness!" he blurted. "What has been done to you?"

After having taken a closer look at it he came to the conclusion: "He must have used drugs!"

"He thrust me to unconsciousness three times," she told him, "and got my female essence to fill three glasses and drained them all. He also fucked me in the asshole about four or five hundred times and even drew out my rectum, about three or four inches in length. To make it go back in, he crouched down and licked and bucked it with his tongue. I thought no one would have touched that filthy thing and felt very grateful to him. As I could do nothing in return for his affection, I asked Saihong to perform the act of lovemaking for me. But his semen refused to come out and I had to let him work on Axiu. He did it with her about half a day, yet still without getting a single drop of his sperm wrenched out. He was so nice to me, how can I repay him for his kindness?"

"You think he was nice to you?" Easterngate growled. "His eating your female essence was actually like sucking the marrow of your bone, and his licking your rectal tube could be as bad as gorging your heart and munching your liver. He was so vicious to you and you still feel grateful to him! What makes me feel really angry is that he dared have sex with Saihong and Axiu. For this insult alone I'll definitely take revenge on him! Now, let me cure your injury first and I'll settle the account with him later."

With this he hurried off. After finding the remedy he needed, he headed for a pharmacy, bought licorice roots and then rushed back home. He decocted the medicinal herbs in water, and when it was done, washed her infected parts with the juice. Jin felt much better after the cleaning.

"How come you know all these things?" she said.

She then washed herself several times. Easterngate soaked a gob of cotton, gently put it into her vagina, and disinfected it for her over and over again. The swelling of her labia went down and the broken skin inside peeled off at once. She felt as refreshed and brisk as before. Seeing her husband being so careful ministering to her wounds, she burst into tears.

"Why are you crying?" Easterngate asked.

"Adultery is a very horrid sin for women," she said, her face streaked with tears. "Nothing can make a man hate his wife more than letting him know that she has had an affair, and he will either kill her or divorce her for her unfaithfulness. But now I myself have become such a monstrous adultress. You have neither killed me nor divorced me. On the contrary, you are afraid that I might die and therefore decocted the medicine for me. You are so in love with me. Is it that I am different from other women, so you are willingly doing me this favour? No, it's just because my sweetheart loves me dearly. You love me dearly but I have returned your love by loving somebody else. Can I still be considered as a human being? I feel too ashamed, too guilty, to face you! I'll hang myself!"

Easterngate took her into his arms, his eyes full of tears.

"Dear heart," he said, "you are an honest and decent woman by nature and it is I who has led you astray. I have been worried about your health so I bought you the medication. But you want to commit suicide! Dear heart, if you kill yourself, I'll follow you! So I beg you not to talk about it any more. Don't you remember what the ancient says, 'Let bygones be bygones'?"

If you want to know whether or not Jin committed suicide, how Easterngate comforted her, and what scheme he used to take revenge on Dali, please read what is told in the next part.

Part II

Our story recommences.

"I hate Dali," Jin said. "He is such a cruel and merciless villain! You are not to be with him again. If he dares come into my sight, mind he not let me bite his flesh off!"

Easterngate laughed. "To hate him is certainly not enough," he said. "We shouldn't let him off so lightly. I'm really cross!"

Jin meditated upon revenge for a moment.

"I have an idea," she said.

"What is it?" he asked.

"He has laid your wife for nothing, so why shouldn't you do the same thing to him? He hasn't married yet, it's true; but he has his mother, a woman who is in her early thirties and has been widowed over ten years. I want to trap this widow into my snare, so that my sweetheart can enjoy her as much as her son did with me. Nothing can make me feel happier than that."

"Actually I got revenge on him for his sodomizing you," Easterngate told her. "When I returned home just now, I saw him lying on the tippler's recliner in the study, sound asleep. I went in and fucked him. No sooner did he wake up than he began serving me, and I could tell that he was miming you in posture and the like, trying to flatter me. He did give me a great deal of pleasure this time; only I was not quite so capable as to pull his rectum out. This I can't but take as a small regret. Now you have a different idea: to set a trap for his mother. I know she is a pretty woman. But to ruin her chastity is something that goes against my conscience and I can't be hard-hearted enough to do that. Besides, you know, his mother is not the type of person you can afford to provoke."

"Darling, you are too kind-hearted," Jin said. "If you are willing to follow my plan, I'll by all means put her at your disposal and you can screw her as much as you like."

Easterngate was curious.

"How can you make that happen?"

"Dali is very afraid of her," she explained. "What you need to do is go to his house and tell Ma that some private school in another region is seeking a teacher and you want to recommend him for that tutorship. Make sure that she will urge him to take the job and then there is nothing he can do but pack up his stuff and set out. Should he mention me, you may say that my cunt has been ripped up and it will take at least two months to heal and will therefore not be available during this period. Thus when you inform him about a two-month temporary teaching position in another area, he surely won't be suspicious of your intention. When the time comes for his departure, I believe he will say that he can't leave his mother alone at home. You should then tell him that it is indeed not good for him to leave his mother alone at home and you can bring her over to our house and we can live together. You and Dali have been buddies for years, visiting each other as often as you could, so I believe his mother won't deny your invitation. When she comes over to stay with us, I'll dispatch you to somewhere else. I have conceived an excellent plan for you, and I guarantee I can make her something certain of your attainment."

"Marvellous! Marvellous!" Easterngate exclaimed. "My former employer in Huzhou wants me to go back to teach and has sent somebody here to invite me. Maybe I should take advantage of this opportunity to recommend Dali, letting him take my place. What do you say?"

"That'd be ideal," she said.

The next morning Easterngate rose early, and after combing his hair and dressing himself up, went to Dali's house. It so happened that Dali was not home. Somebody fond of male love had coaxed and cajoled him into spending the night outside. Easterngate went straight in to pay his respects to Madam Ma, who invited him to tea, and drank and chatted with him.

"Mr. Yao," she said, "where did you come from? Have you seen Dali?"

"He didn't come to my study yesterday," he replied. "I thought he was home, so I came here looking for him. A good private school in Huzhou is seeking a teacher, offering a remuneration of thirty taels. They want me to take that position and have sent someone for me. Unfortunately I have some private matters to deal with and can't go there now. The job market doesn't look good lately and rarely have I seen an opening in private schools. Today I have come here just for this matter and not for anything else, and I would like to tell you that I have recommended my Younger Brother to teach for me."

Ma got very excited upon hearing this.

"Damned wretch!" she could not help bursting out. "He is really making me cross! You probably don't know that my son has recently hung around with two shady bachelors. One of them lives in front of the Temple of Jade Flower and his name is Chang Fen. Since his name and the name of the Prince of Yue, Changfen, are homophonic, people call him 'The Transgressive Young Man of the Propriety,' a sobriquet based on the gossip about that prince.[20] The other one, also gay, is the son of Jin the Inspector of Rivers and Canals. He lives right beside the Labyrinth and is known among his friends as Jin Ai [meaning "narrow"]. 'The fly likes staying in a filthy *narrow* place' as the saying goes, so they gave him the nickname 'Jin the Fly.' I'm sure Dali must be with these two bachelors now. It has been some time since I noticed that he loafed around, and I was just now wondering how to get him a job at a private school so that he can do something serious and grow up mature and steady. I just don't know where to go to secure one for him and here you come with this good news. Isn't it wonderful!"

Easterngate, however, was rather droopy to hear this.

"Chang Fen happens to be my close neighbour," he said, "and Jin the Fly my nephew by marriage. I know these two young fellows and they are indeed bachelors. I'm worried that Younger Brother might begrudge parting company with them."

"You don't have to worry about that," Ma said. "He'll go if I want him to. Thank you anyway."

"When Younger Brother is gone," Easterngate went on, "Mother might feel lonely at home, and moreover, there'll be nobody helping Mother with water, firewood, and that sort of thing. Considering these inconveniences, I would like to invite you to stay with us. My wife can keep you company day and night, and you can also take care of her when I am away from home."

"Oh, no!" Ma declined. "That would be too much trouble! But I appreciate your kind offer and will discuss it with my son to see what he'll say about it."

Dali, however, did not come back until after Easterngate had left. Ma's face fell as she saw him report in. "Don't think no one knows that you spent the night with those two bachelors!" she said. "Why didn't you go to the study yesterday? Just now Elder Brother Yao came to see me, saying that a good private school in Huzhou has an opening and he has recommended you for that position. Now, go pack your things and get yourself ready for departure!"

Seeing his mother had discovered his frivolous pursuits, Dali felt rather ashamed. He flushed with embarrassment.

"Well, on my part, that should be no problem," he said insincerely in order to conceal his discomfiture. "Only I'm afraid that you might feel lonely at home by yourself."

"Never mind," she said. "Elder Brother Yao said I can move over to their house and stay with them during your absence. So I won't feel lonely there. You just go your way!"

Dali now realized that his mother was serious and there was actually not much choice left for him. But he really did not want to part with Jin, nor was he willing to separate from his two bachelor pals.

"Surely it's good to live with them," he said. "You can save money, and on top of that, will have somebody keeping you company. But the problem is I am not good at teaching."

Ma flared up.

"This is a career opportunity for you!" she fumed. "Studying and then teaching, most men take this path. I have spent seventeen or eighteen years bringing you up and if you are man enough, you should have already begun earning some money to support your parent!"

"Please don't get angry, Mom," Dali apologized. "Your son now understands the importance of teaching and will be setting off tomorrow or the day after."

He took leave of her and hurried toward Easterngate's.

"Elder Brother, did you blame me?" he panted, seeing Easterngate standing outside on the porch. "Otherwise I just don't understand why you made my mother urge me to go to that faraway place?"[21]

Easterngate grabbed him with his hand and pulled him inside. "Yesterday," he said, after sitting himself on a chair, "I came back home and saw your sister-in-law lying in bed with her pussy swollen. I laughed at her and also praised you for your unusual power. How could you say that I blamed you? Only it so happened that somebody came from afar visiting me yesterday, telling me that a good private school in Huzhou is seeking an instructor. That is the school where I was formerly employed and this year I'll have to handle some private matters and can't go there to teach myself. So I have recommended Younger Brother. The salary is quite good and you can sure make some money if you are willing to accept the offer. I never thought that my good intention would be doubted!"

"Elder Brother, thank you for your kindness," Dali said. "But to be frank, I really don't want to be apart from Sister-in-Law."

"This is something I need to explain to you," said Easterngate. "You screwed your sister-in-law half a day and a whole night, breaking the skin of her vagina and causing its lips to swell. Now they have begun festering and running with pus, and will take at least two months to be completely cured. Even if you stay here, you can't do it with her anyway. That's why I suggest that you go take the job and forget about her for the time being. When you come back home two months from now, you'll surely enjoy a greater pleasure."

Dali, upon hearing this, made a hurried obeisance by cupping one hand in the other before his chest. "Elder Brother, you are so kind-hearted! I would feel guilty if I refused to listen to you. I will let Sister-in-Law take a good rest for some time. Have you, by the way, asked her if she is afraid of me?"

"Your sister-in-law has a lecherous beaver," Easterngate replied. "Only an iron prick like yours can make her feel satisfied. But now she so hurts down there with the bad sores that she has to give up sexual enjoyment temporarily. So go on your trip, Younger Brother. Don't worry about your family. I'll bring your mother over to our house and we'll both take care of her."

"You are very generous to me," said Dali, "and I'm sorry to put you to so much trouble just on my account."

"Please don't feel that way," Easterngate smiled. "Sister-in-Law has slept with you so she is just like your wife. Your mother, then, is just like her own mother-in-law. A daughter-in-law has the duty to support and assist her mother-in-law, so you shouldn't think that it is an extra burden for us."

"With such an explanation," Dali said, "you have virtually left me with no choice, but thank you for your kindness.

All right, I'll go home now to pack my baggage."

He took his leave and went back home.

Jin had actually been standing behind the wall as they talked and had heard every word they had said.

"This crazy beast wants to screw me again!" she cursed when Dali had left.

She then pressed Easterngate, "Go get his mother!"

Once again Easterngate set out for Dali's house. When he arrived there, he saw Dali already putting things in his bags. He went in to invite Ma.

"As soon as he is gone, I'll come over," Ma replied. "But I'm afraid that I might give you too much trouble."

"We are as close as flesh and blood and it is really nothing to us," Easterngate said. He urged her to pack her clothes and quilts, and Ma did as she was told.

Dali said to his mother, "I'm ready to depart now."

"All right," she said. "When you are alone there, you should apply yourself to study. Don't drink too much, nor go whoring. I'll see to it that I find you a beautiful girl to be your wife."

"Yes," Dali answered.

He then said to Easterngate, "Elder Brother, this is a very good arrangement. With my mother staying at your home, I shall have nothing to worry about. This year you helped me get this job and I feel very happy. I'm really grateful for your kindness. I'll come back to see you in two months."

"I'll look forward to getting together with you," said Easterngate.

Dali then lowered his voice, murmuring, "Elder Brother, I want to go to your house with you to say goodbye to Sister-in-Law."

"You'd better not," Easterngate disuaded him. "Your

sister-in-law is laid up with that ailment, and besides, your mother is going now as well. I'll send your regards to her for you. Now you are going to stay away for sixty days and you should husband your energy during this period. I hope you'll be able to give her a good fuck on your return."

"Whatever you say, I'll listen to you," Dali warbled. "Please send my warmest regards to her and also remind her to get things ready for me when I come back home."

"That's no problem," Easterngate promised.

After bidding farewell to his mother and Elder Brother, Dali set out for Huzhou, with his page-boy carrying the baggage for him.

Our story goes that Easterngate hired a sedan for Ma and her maid Little Pretty and brought them to his house. Jin put on makeup before going out to greet them as they arrived. Since she still felt a little fatigue, she had drunk some *ginseng* water beforehand.

Upon seeing Ma, she said, "Long time no see, Mama."

Ma returned, "Many thanks for inviting me to stay with you. But I feel rather uneasy about giving you this trouble."

"I hope I will be a good host and make you feel at home!" Jin said, smiling.

"You certainly are," said Ma.

Jin bade Saihong and Axiu to set the table. Soon food and wine were spread out on it, along with various kinds of fruit on plates. They sat down to eat, without Easterngate's company. Jin sat at one side and Ma took the seat of honour, looking as if they were mother-in-law and daughter-in-law for real.

"Now that I live at your place," Ma said, "we should eat ordinary meals as you would eat everyday by yourselves. Never ever again prepare such a feast just on my account!"

"No problem, Mama," Jin replied. "We'll just eat home-ly food every day as you suggest."

She then had a room tidied up, where Ma spent her night.

The next morning at dawn Easterngate got up. "I'm going to the countryside to visit my relatives," he pronounced. "It'll take fifteen days or so."

He deliberately said goodbye to Ma as Jin had bidden him to. In fact, he did not go anywhere, just hiding himself in a room which was relatively secluded. Without seeing him in the house, Ma thought that he was indeed gone.

In the evening Jin came into Ma's room.

"My husband is away and I'm feeling lonely," she said. "Could I sleep with you tonight, Mama? I'd be happy if you allow me to."

"That's certainly very good," Ma said.

In a low voice Jin bade Saihong to go to Easterngate and keep him company for the night. She then called Axiu to prepare supper and bring it into the guest room. When the dinner was ready, the two of them, sitting face to face, began to eat. Ma had only a little capacity for wine, about the amount of one cup at maximum. At Jin's persistent urge, she forced herself to drink six or seven cups.

"Sister Yao, I have had more than I can hold," she said, rather tipsy. "I'd like to go to sleep now."

"Fine," Jin replied. "I'll be with you after I clear off the table."

No sooner had she finished than she began to disrobe Ma, who felt rather ill at ease. "Please don't bother, Sister," she said.

She undressed herself and got into the bed.

"Let's sleep opposite!" she suggested.

"But I'd like to have a chat with you, Mama," Jin cajoled

her. "It's much more convenient if we sleep in the same direction."

Under the influence, Ma was unable to resist the temptation. She murmured, "For the last ten or more years, no one has ever shared a bed with me in this way. I had no expectation that tonight I would sleep with Sister head to head!"

Tonight, Jin thought, I must set this dame astir.

"Mama, why don't you take off your underwear?" she asked. "As for me, I can't fall asleep with so much as a stitch on."

"I would certainly like to," Ma said. "Only I feel shy with nothing on in front of other people."

"We are both women," said Jin. "There actually isn't anything between us you should feel shy about."

Upon her insistence, Ma removed the remaining petticoat until she had had no clothes left. She turned toward the inner side to sleep, wrapping herself tight with her quilt.

"Tonight is a little cold," Jin fluttered. "I'd like to share your quilt with you, Mama, if you don't mind."

With this she squeezed herself underneath Ma's bedclothes.

Ma found it difficult to push her away and had to let Jin snuggle close to her. Suddenly, she heaved a sigh.

"Mama, are you feeling all right?" Jin asked. "Why are you sighing?"

"I am sighing, Sister, simply because your sleeping with me has reminded me of my late husband."

"Oh really! Do you still miss him? When he was alive, you must have led a happy life, I suppose?"

"We had been married for only four years and then he was taken by death," Ma told her.

"More than ten years have passed since your husband

left you. I wonder if you still think about him at night?"

"How can I forget him?" Ma replied, grinning. "But this is Fate, which I have to endure."

Jin snickered. "Why do you think of him, may I ask? Probably not because of lack of clothes or food, I gather?"

"Time to sleep, Sister," Ma cracked a smile. "No more questions!"

Jin did not dare ask her again. Before long Ma fell into a sound slumber.

"Mama, Mama," Jin called twice, without hearing any response.

Gently, she let her hand run down Ma's belly to her groin, to feel her privates. They were rather fleshy, covered with tufts of fine hair all around. She moved on, further downward till she touched her vulva, which, shielded by two soft, plump labia, protruded slightly. The slit was very smooth, and she could feel there was not even the slightest trace of wetness in there.

This is no doubt the most excellent pussy I can find for my husband, she thought. I must try my best to create an opportunity for him so that he can make love to her to his heart's desire!

She then dug a finger into Ma's furrow and frigged it lightly. Ma let out a low moan, then lay on her back, with one leg shot up and the other stretched to one side.

"Mama," Jin called once again.

There was no answer.

She spat some spittle onto her fingers and rubbed it into Ma's twat. She slathered more when it opened up, making her outer folds soaking wet. Ma was still sound asleep. Seeing no sign of her wake up, Jin stuck a finger into her hole and stirred, applying more spit to its interior walls. Now Ma's vagina, inside and out, was all wet.

Jin had a *mianling*, a vibrator, which she had tucked in a handkerchief. She undid the handkerchief and took it out, waiting for her companion to come alive.

I might as well give her a try now, she thought.

She reached down between her legs, with the ball in hand, and then pressed it into the slippery snatch with alacrity. To block the bulb-like gadget from rolling out, she gave a light pull at Ma's arched leg and got it straight, and then closed Ma's thighs up and set her own on top of them, fixing them. Ma, in her dreamy state, felt her vagina throbbingly itchy and sore. Her fluid started flowing out like pee, spreading all over the sheet. The *mianling* kept rolling inside, so stimulating that she was gradually awakened from her sleep.

"What a tingling sensation!" she mumbled.

She would have liked to move herself about, but with her legs being solidly pressed, she just could not do so.

"Oh dear!" she murmured once again, and kept murmuring a few more times before finally waking up.

"Sister," she called.

"Yes?"

"I want to get up."

"It's very late now," Jin said. "You'd better not loiter around in such darkness."

"But I feel like moving about," Ma insisted.

"Why, Mama?"

"Sister, your legs are weighing upon mine and I feel very uncomfortable," she said.

Jin smiled. "I'm drunk and don't have the least bit of energy for moving myself about. Just push me off yourself, please!"

Ma gave her a hard shove, trying to remove her legs. Jin, however, held on, sticking to her as close as before.

"Sister," said Ma, "your legs seem to have taken root on my body and I just can't push them off."

"My goodness," Jin deliberately burst out, "you have made the sheet very wet here!"

Upon hearing this, Ma broke into an awkward grin.

"I'm having a little pain down there," she said.

"But how could your fluid come out with *pain*?" Jin questioned, laughing. "Perhaps it is not pain, but a *twinge* or something, I suppose?"

"To be frank with you, I do feel a little sore," Ma simpered. "But I can't figure out what has caused this soreness."

"Do you also have a tingling feeling?" Jin asked.

"How do you know?" Ma was shocked. "You must have put something in there, haven't you? I do feel some titillation below."

"Mama, I have a little appliance called a *mianling*," Jin said. "I myself call it Cockbeater. This little thing can provide me with as much pleasure as I want. Mama has long been living to the exclusion of this kind of enjoyment and just now I was a little naughty, inserting my Cockbeater into that place."

"Goodness me!" Ma cried. "You have been playing a trick on me! Could you please remove your legs? I want to take it out."

"Mama, let it be there a little longer and you'll have a greater enjoyment."

With this she shook Ma's hips a couple of times, setting the *mianling* running wildly inside. Prudish as she was, Ma found it hard to remain unperturbed with such stimulation.

"Stop rocking me, Sister!" she shouted. "You are making me feel too sore to stand it."

Jin, however, did not take out the *mianling* immediately.

I can tell that this dame has been sexed up, she thought.

She then said, "Is there any other thing as good as this gadget, a tickler that can give you hundreds and hundreds of strokes and set you atingle so much that you'd feel as if you were coupling with a real man?"

"Indeed, this cock is not bad," Ma replied, laughing. "You are right, Sister. We certainly can't find a man capable of sticking a woman so many times." She felt quite aroused as she uttered these indecorous words, experiencing a firing-up below.

Jin broke into giggles.

"You had never made use of this thing when your husband was alive?" she queried. "To my knowledge, any man below the mark can easily give a woman five or six hundred thrusts, and a thousand thrusts are not unusual for ordinary men. As for those mighty and strong guys, they may even thrust a woman over ten thousand times, I believe."

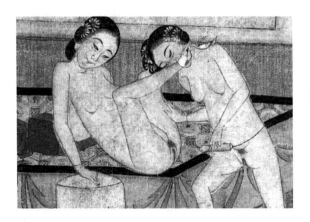

"That sounds incredible," Ma disagreed. "Let me tell you something of my own experience. When I married into the Zhao household, I was only about fifteen years old, and I still remember how my husband made love to me the first night we slept together. He first rubbed some spit on that place, and then prodded his finger and dug into it several times. The pain was so sharp I squealed. He then produced his thing and brushed it against my labes. No sooner had it touched my skin than he came and broke down. Later, he frigged me every night with his fingers and my hole gradually opened up. Still our sex was a quick business and he could only give me one thrust or two before getting off. This lasted about a year. Afterwards he got into the habit of applying his spit to that place before putting it in. Having more stamina now, he could sometimes give me three or four strokes, and sometimes five or six. Once he thrust into me thirteen or fourteen times, the maximum strokes I have ever had. I asked him why he had usually been capable of only one thrust or two, but this time he could keep doing it as many as thirteen or fourteen times? He replied, 'Most men give seven or eight thrusts, and some only two to three. It is virtually impossible to find another one who can thrust thirteen or fourteen times as I did to you.' Now Sister is talking about a thousand. If I am not mistaken, you probably refer to the total thrusts of a hundred intercourses as a whole?"

Jin laughed. "Poor Mama, you have been taken in," she said. "Life is short and we should seize time to enjoy pleasures. That organ of your husband's, as you described just now, belongs actually to the type of 'shedding-tears-in-front-of-the-gate' or 'submitting-an-invitation-like-a-shot.' The cocks of this kind, even when standing up, are not very hard. They might be stiff enough to enter a woman, but can't give her as much pleasure as she wants. Mama, you are unlucky, having spent half of your lifetime without tasting some real delight."

"Please take that thing out," Ma said. "I feel itchy inside."

"Don't move," Jin persisted. "Just keep it in there and you'll soon like it."

Ma, at this moment, was getting high, her fluids starting to ooze out.

Jin went on. "One thing I don't quite understand. Your husband was a sexual impotent and how come he died so young?"

"That had something to do with me," Ma explained. "After having given birth to my son at the age of sixteen, I was no longer tight below as I had been before, so he didn't need to apply spit before entering me. He then often did it with me and I never rejected him. Every time he came, he would unload a huge amount and his hands and feet would turn cold. Later, we coupled almost every night and I began enjoying some pleasures in that place. But he had no staying power. No sooner did I have some pleasure than he would come, and then his penis would quickly shrink regardless of my unsatisfaction. Since he did it with me so often, he grew weaker and weaker, and to make the things worse, he even started having wet dreams at night. He was no longer able to stiffen as frequently as before and whenever I found it hard, I would stuff it inside, with me straddling atop him. However, he could only withstand two to three bounces, and then he would say that he had come and I had to scramble down. Finally, he developed comsumption. Though he could still achieve erection when he was aroused, he came even more quickly than before. He ended up ejaculating blood, and fainted and at length died. It was I who made him fall sick and die, so how could I not miss him?"

"That was not your fault, Mama," Jin comforted her. "Being a woman, we have a pussy and that is our asset. It will itch, which makes our tongue drool; it will tingle, which teases us into moaning. Naturally we need a cock that can buck and stick as forcefully as we want it to. I myself was often laid by my husband and he never failed to give me fun in intercourse. I have a cousin, who has often carried on with me. When I dated him and there was no one around, he would do it with me, to be sure. His endowment – let me not talk about his other strengths – is amazing. It can drive in to the hilt and buck the heart of my cunt until I can't bear the rapture. To be candid with you, I once even lost consciousness because of the overwhelming ecstacy. When I came to, I found myself tingling all over and the jollies of soreness coming one wave after another inside my pelvis, making my red fluids gush forth without cease. It was really a great enjoyment!"

"Sister, how could you do such a thing?" Ma smiled dis-approvingly.

"Well, this can help maintain our good health," Jin said. "A woman will fall ill sooner or later if her spouse is of the type of 'shedding-tears-in-front-of-the-gate.'"

"Really?" Ma was startled. "What illness will she have then?"

"The man whose ejaculation is fast can't make his woman's *yin* and *yang* intermingle," Jin told her. "If the woman has too much *yin* inside her body without disposing of it promptly, she'll be struck down by a malady related to an internal blockage. She won't get well unless she gets rid of her surplus *yin* inside."

"But how can she get rid of it?" Ma asked.

"Nothing can help her get rid of it but a man's cock," Jin said. "She must let a man work her hard enough until she feels that jolts of delight are running over her entire body. Only after having had such intercourse will she be cured of her illness."

Though saying nothing, Ma actually felt quite aroused, what with the provocative words she had heard and with the *mianling* that had been trolling around inside.

Jin went on. "The cousin I mentioned to you just now is a handsome young man. When my husband is away, I often invite him over to spend a night with me. I might as well invite him over tomorrow night to let Mama sleep with him."

"How can I do that?" Ma protested, with a smile.

"Tomorrow night I'll blow out the light before letting him in," Jin said. "I'll sleep with him first and you can wait for me on the other bed. After a while, I'll say I'm going to urinate and let you replace me. Make sure you make little noise as you get into his bed and say nothing during the intercourse, lest he find out that it is a different person. As soon as he is finished, I'll sneak back to take your place and you go retire in your own bed. At that time, I believe, you'll have felt fully satisfied. Mama, isn't it wondrous to enjoy a pleasure without exposing your identity? Your good name will be kept intact, but by taking advantage of this opportunity, you'll be able to get rid of some potential illness that may bring serious harm to your health."

Ma hesitated. "For the last thirteen years," she said, "I have been living in widowhood and I find it hard to break this precept."

"To remain in widowhood is not easy," Jin laughed. "For three or four years it may be all right, but a longer period of celibacy will surely make the woman feel ill at ease. Each year in the second and third months, when flowers are in bloom and weather is getting warm, she'll feel lethargic and tired. Her body will be cold one moment and hot the next, her cheeks red with internal heat and her loins assailed by the spasms of soreness. These are the symptoms of her yearning for a man, which she might be unaware of herself. For a young widow in her twenties, with her sap and vigour unweakened, she can still sleep well at night without being much affected by this lovesickness. But when she is getting older, over thirty or forty years of age, owing to her flagging vitality as well as her stronger sexual desire, she'll have troubled insomnia. No matter how cosy she is with the quilt hugging her, she'll toss and turn in bed, feeling that something is missing. Summer is even worse. Taking a bath, she may dig into her slit by accident, sending shivers all over her body. Mosquitos are particularly annoying. Their buzzing noise and irritating stings, when exacerbated by the streams of sweat that tickle and hurt that sensitive part between her thighs, will often turn her sleep into something of unbearable nightmares. With the arrival of autumn, cold wind begins to blow. Couples, their windows closed, will sit together drinking and making love to each other. However, she is alone by herself; no one keeps her company but a lone moon, which can only give her its cold light as comfort. At that time, she might feel sad even to hear crickets' chirping and the whack of beating clothes. Nothing can excite her more than the hallucination that she is being embraced by someone in sleep. To while away time in winter is even more difficult. There is not much fun in sitting before the fireplace all day long just by herself. But in those windy, snowing days, what else can she do?

Sleeping certainly won't help her feel any better. The quilt is cold, and its worn-out padding and thin slipcover can't bring her much warmth. Wearing thin clothes, she has to cuddle up to herself so as not to touch some ice-cold spots. She only wishes she could hold a man in an embrace to warm herself, even if this man is an old codger!

"Thinking that she has been widowed only a few years, she is now not so confident that she can survive another forty or fifty years and live up to her old age. Remarriage will bring her into disrepute. To date someone on the sly, however, will be even more scandalous if the partner is not discreet enough to keep their secret. But with my arrangement, Mama, you don't have to worry about such a problem, for you'll just be a stand-in, taking my place in bed with him for a night. You should avail yourself of this opportunity and I believe, as you are being vigorously thrust by him, you'll enjoy a pleasure that even the *mianling* can't give to you, the pleasure that you'll feel is worth spending your life for. Of course, you don't want my husband to know about it. Trust me. I'll never betray you! Your son shouldn't be a problem either. I won't gossip about you in front of him and he has no way of knowing what you do, good or bad. So have a try as I have suggested! I only hope you won't fall in love with him so as to be unwilling to part with him and give him back to me."

Ma laughed. "Sister, you are so cajoling I feel I can hardly resist your seduction. I'll do as you say despite the wish of my late husband. Though I have lived more than thirty years, I have never before enjoyed such a great pleasure as the thing you stuffed down there is giving to me, let alone the more stimulating delight that only a thousand strokes can provide. I am not too old for amusement, anyway. But what if I get pregnant? That makes me feel frightened. Could you please tell him to pull his thing out by the time he is going to spend, Sister?"

"Mama, the most enjoyable time is when the man is about to come," Jin said, smiling. "His dick will grow bigger and redder, and will fill the vagina without even leaving one centimetre of room. At that time his hard thrusts can give the woman such great pleasure that she'll feel she is going to pass out. Mama, you don't have to worry about pregnancy. I still have some contraceptive pills that I used when I was a maiden. You can take some if you want."

Ma felt her passions aflame.

"Fancy, I am going to have a real man who is even more capable than this Cockbeater!" she exclaimed. "I regret that I married the wrong person and wasted ten more years of my youth. Still, it's not too late. I should seize this opportunity to enjoy myself to the full!"

Hearing this, Jin slid her hand down again and rocked Ma's pussy like mad. The ball in there began rolling ferociously, producing tingling waves so strong that Ma felt she could hardly bear it. She jerked her legs in spite of herself and broke loose from Jin's compression. The *mianling* popped out from within.

"What a pleasure, Sister!" she screamed. "I would like to take a look at this rolling gadget."

She grabbed hold of the ball as it rolled out, gazing at it for a while.

"It's round," she said. "But I wonder how it can rotate inside?"

"This *mianling* was imported from Burma," Jin explained. "Inside it has mercury, with the gold as you see wrapping it up outside. In making the wrappings, the artisan applied a thin layer of gold first and heated it, and then applied the second layer, and then the third layer. This one consists of seven layers of gold altogether. Since the mercury keeps flowing inside, it dashes against the gold, making the ball vibrate and roll constantly."

"Sister," Ma chuckled, "you must have used it often, I guess?"

"This is just a dead treasure," said Jin. "I prefer a live one, the man's cock."

With this she put the *mianling* back into Ma, who was no longer reserved as she had been before. Being horny, and also with the intention of satisfying her desire, she let Jin feel her crotch as she pleased, making no attempt to remove her hand.

"Mama," Jin said, "if I didn't secretly insert my Cock-beater into your cunt, I believe you would remain continent the rest of your days, not knowing any sexual pleasures of this sort."

"Absolutely," Ma said.

Day broke after they had played for some time. They got up. Jin called Saihong to prepare breakfast and Axiu to help Ma to dress her hair. All the while, Ma was beaming with joy.

Jin went to the sequestered room where Easterngate stayed.

"My lordy," she said, "you have been enjoying the whole night doing it with Saihong! Did you know how hard I was working for you all this time in order to get hold of the woman you want? Now I have got everything settled and you can expect a tryst tonight!"

"How did you make it, honey?" Easterngate asked, smiling.

"Let me tell you later how I baited her. "Tonight, around

the second watch, I'll blow out the light and have Saihong invite Mr. Guo. At her invitation you come over to sleep with me first. When I want to rise, you just let me do so, so that I can let Dali's mother substitute me. But you should pretend that you notice nothing different and keep working hard. She may want to get up when you are going to spend. Just let her go, and I'll return to sleep with you again before you leave for your own room. Isn't this a flawless arrangement?"

"Thank you, honey," said Easterngate. "I'll surely do as you told me. I have just now taken an aphrodisiac, which can help hold off ejaculation and make the endowment virile. So even if I have to deal with a hundred women tonight, it shouldn't be a problem for me."

"Excellent!" Jin said. "But why didn't you ever take this drug before when you made love with me?"

"Well," Easterngate defended himself, "I just found it a moment ago after a special search."

"Never mind," said Jin.

She went back to Ma's room.

"The cousin I mentioned to you last night will be coming tonight," she pronounced.

"This thing," Ma stressed, "we can only do it this way, the way we make a deal with the people from a different place."

"What does that mean?" Jin asked.

"I mean this isn't a good deal," she said.

They spent half a day in the room chattering and joking. Jin took out the erotic paintings, a bundle of them, which Easterngate had collected, and spread them out one by one for Ma to look at. Ma cackled after contemplating a picture that was quite funny.

"Isn't this way of having sex interesting!" she quipped.

"You can try it too when he comes to keep you company tonight," Jin suggested. "I can guarantee your pleasure if you do as I told you last night. You ought to thank me for my advice."

Ma laughed. "I can, of course, do as you said, but I am afraid that may make me end up as a woman of bad name!"

"No, you won't!" Jin said.

They ate lunch and then some snacks in the afternoon. Soon it was dinner time. Axiu lit the lamps while Saihong busied herself bringing food in.

"Mama," Jin asked, "have you put away the Cockbeater that you used last night?"

"Yes. Could you please lend it to me?"

Jin laughed. "You may not cherish this dead treasure any more when you have the live one to play with," she said.

She came out of the room after bantering for a while and said to Saihong in a low voice, "Tonight, around the second watch,[22] I'll have you invite Mr. Guo. You should then bring our master in, understand?"

Having so instructed her, she went back in and said to Ma, "My cousin came to see me just now and I have asked him to join me in my room around the second watch tonight. Mama, you should be there by that time and sleep on the couch nearby. When you hear me say I'm going to pee, just climb over to take my place. Don't you think this is an excellent plan? It won't get you caught like those who steal the bell by covering their ears."

Ma laughed, nodding her head.

"Only I feel rather embarrassed," she said.

"Take it easy," Jin comforted her. "I'm not a prude, and besides, you have done nothing illicit before and should enjoy yourself tonight to your heart's content. Nobody knows it but me. Even the two maids will take it for granted that it's I who is having a tryst with him. Since my cousin and the maids are completely in the dark, why shouldn't you make the best of it by taking advantage of their ignorance?"

"You have set my lust aflame," Ma grinned. "Well, I'll just let you manipulate things the way you want."

After dinner, Jin pulled Ma into her chamber and bade Little Pretty to go back to sleep in her room. Axiu had re-arranged the master bedroom beforehand and there were two beds now, both with bedclothes, ready for serving. Jin invited Ma to choose a bed for herself.

"Sister," Ma said, out of politeness, "you should sleep on the big one."

Jin did not decline. They both laughed as they went to retire. Unable to fall asleep, Ma tossed and turned over and over again in her bed. She could hear no sound, with all being quiet and still outside. All of sudden, the drum tower tolled the second watch and she heard Jin call out to Saihong: "Go invite Mr. Guo. Be quick about it!"

The maid no doubt understood whom she was referring to. In one breath she blew out the light and made her way to that quiet isolated cubicle where her master stayed. At her "invitation," Easterngate swiftly sneaked to their bed-room. Ma had jumped up when hearing his footsteps. She saw the man stride straight in to the big bed.

With her tone deliberately kept low, Jin said to Easterngate, "He has been home recently so I couldn't see you. I have sure as hell missed you!"

He made no reply and let her rattle on for a while. Soon the bed started giving off creaks as they engaged in action.

"Sweetheart," Jin moaned, "you are thrusting into me really well!"

Upon hearing these stimulating words Ma felt so aroused that her fluid oozed out. She had to insert the *mianling* into her vagina and frig it while waiting.

Jin groaned once more, her voice affectedly sweet, "Oh my dear heart, I feel so good!"

Now Ma was worked up to a fever pitch. She bit her finger, trying to quench her raging passion. She is immersed in rapture, she thought, and has probably forgotten that she should take a pee now. How can I endure one more minute?

On an impulse she touched the bell that was hung on the bed.

"Sweet, wait a moment," she heard Jin say to the man. "Please excuse me to use the toilet now."

Upon hearing this, Ma hastily descended from her couch. Jin, having alighted from her bed, went to the night-stool to urinate. When she had finished, she came over to pull her companion and gave her a push on the shoulders. Ma had by now completely undressed, and without much reluctance, quickly got into the other bed. Jin then climbed to the small couch to sleep.

No sooner had Ma slipped in than Easterngate, who knew who she was, started his onslaught at the slit between her thighs. Grace in movement, Ma raised her legs and opened them at once to let him work his way inside, making not the slightest sound. Easterngate pressed hard on her belly, kissing her, and then forced his tongue into her mouth. After she let it in, he began to ram its tip against the base of hers, once, twice, until she in return stuck hers into his mouth. Easterngate gripped it fast, and kept hold of it while sticking her cunt. Having received a hundred or more thrusts in succession, Ma felt a good tingling sensation never experienced before and she could not help reaching out to clasp him in a tight embrace and wrapping her legs around his waist. Easterngate sensed that she was inflamed and deliberately sucked her tongue hard enough to emit loud slurps.

What a treat she is enjoying! Jin thought, listening intently to everything that went on. Funny it has not yet occurred to her that I'm playing a trick on her!

Easterngate had grown rather steamy now. He strove harder than ever, making the bed rock and squawk without cease. Ma was unable to bear his thrusts and let out cries of "aaah, aaah." Hearing this, Easterngate raised her feet over his shoulders, and bucked and pounded her with all his might for four or five hundred times until her secretion gushed forth in a torrent.

"What a pleasure! What a pleasure!" Ma shrieked. "You are tickling me to death!"

Feeling that he was going to come, Easterngate did not dare move again. He puffed a breath to keep from ejaculating. Ma was having an awful itch in there and gradually lost control of herself. She wriggled her hips up and down, squeezing and clutching his dick as much as she could.

"Darling boy, why don't you move?" she pressed.

At her entreaty, Easterngate had to pull himself together and gave her another fifty or sixty thrusts.

"Oh, my dear heart," she exclaimed, "I'm dying! And I'd content myself with dying so happily!"

Easterngate noticed that she had become very wanton. She may not care now even if she finds out who I am, he deliberated.

He then asked, "Are you enjoying it?"

In the tremor of her excitement, Ma paid no attention at all to his voice and replied, "Yes, I am, Elder Brother. Could you stick in a little more, please?"

Rather than doing what she asked him to, he withdrew himself, letting only the tip of his penis brush lightly against her vulva. Ma was so turned on by his scrapings that she thought no more of her being a widow. She perked up her rump toward him, and the more he backed out, the higher she raised it. With such a hot pursuit, Easterngate had to plunge in to the hilt once again and pump her as hard as he could. After three hundred or more thrusts, Ma tingled all over and gritted her teeth aloud. Easterngate felt that she was about to climax and gave her some sideways attacks and then ferociously stirred inside for a while.

"You are thrilling me to death!" Ma cried. "But mind you don't mention it to anybody! Otherwise my good name would be ruined."

"So it's you!" Easterngate said, keeping thrusting. "Sorry about having mistaken you for somebody else."

He pretended to draw back. But Ma held him tight.

"You have done it with me half a night already," she said, "so what is this apology for? Just keep doing it as before!"

"Mama, you are betraying your true colors!" Jin burst out from her couch. "Well then, it's not necessary for me to hide any more nor for you to leave."

With this she came over to their bed.

Ma spoke her mind to her, "Shameful as it is, Sister, I can't give it another thought. I know I have been cajoled, but I feel very happy now!"

"That's good," Jin said.

While Easterngate resumed his pumping as vigorously

as before, Jin leaned over to plant a kiss on Ma's mouth.

"Are you feeling good, Mama?" she asked.

"Nothing has made me feel better than this most delightful enjoyment," Ma replied. "After all, it's not an unprofitable venture and I do feel satisfied."

She then jutted out the tip of her tongue, letting her companion lap and suck it as she liked.

"Look," said Jin, "I'm sucking your tongue for you!"

"Don't foul things up here!" Easterngate rumbled at her. "Wait until I get done with her and then I'll be with you, all right?"

"As you say," Ma answered.

She reached out to hold Easterngate's waist. To let her set her feet over his shoulders, Easterngate had to crouch down a little bit. He then straightened his back and sheathed his hard-on with a device decorated with some goose feathers before engaging her in a fierce bout. After a thousand or more thrusts, Ma screamed, "What a rapturous delight! What a rapturous delight! I'm dying!"

"Mama," Jin said, "you are probably tired, aren't you? Have you spent?"

"No, I'm not tired yet," she replied. "I want to continue to do it with him, I mean, with you!"

"It seems you are highly interested in this sort of thing," Easterngate observed. "How did you endure years of loneliness before?"

"To tell you the truth," Ma said, "I dug in with my fingers when I had an itch down there. Sure enough, my own digging and rubbing can't be compared with the lovemaking you are performing on me."

"Enough of this idle talk!" Jin interrupted. "Keep riding Mama hard!"

Easterngate, with his passion being in full flow, gave Ma five hundred thrusts ceaselessly without even pausing to catch his breath. Jin grew excited as she looked on from the bedside. She reached out to feel his genitals.

"Your goose-feathered balls are striking her turd gate with each thrust, causing it to swell now!" she said, laughing.

Ma said nothing in response, still squirming her hips frantically and meanwhile moving herself further upward to press against his pelvis. In fast tempo Easterngate thrust into her another two hundred times.

"I'm going to spend," he said.

"Good!" Jin cheered on.

"Go ahead if you want to," Ma agreed. "I have had enough."

Easterngate started anew his full-strength thrusting, which he did as quickly as possible for about a hundred times or so, followed then by more furious bucking and grinding, with his shaft plunged in all the way to the base.

Ma was worked up to the height of her passion.

"Sweetheart, I'm tingling so much I can't bear it any more!" she screeched.

Jin warned, "Hey, don't cry so loud!"

Easterngate was no longer able to restrain himself. He blew his wad inside her, his dick jerking uncontrollably twice. Ma clutched him tightly with her legs.

"Are you satisfied?" he asked. "What do you think of my prowess?"

"My husband never gave me more than ten thrusts," Ma replied, "so I had no expectation that the pleasure I was to enjoy tonight would be so overwhelming. As long as I am alive, I'll stay with you! I really can't bear the separation from my darling boy! I'm now only thirty years old, not looking too old. I want to marry you. Could you please tell me your age and whether you have a spouse at home?"

"I'm also thirty years old," said Easterngate. "So it's settled: I'll take you as my wife!"

Jin laughed. "But where will you dump me then?" she asked.

Ma, still unaware that the man was Easterngate, counselled him: "After I have married you, I'll allow you to carry on with her as she visits me. As for our relationship, I'm going to tell my son straightforward that I can't remain a widow any more and am considering remarriage. On your part, you should ready yourself for our wedding ceremony. What do you think?"

"I appreciate your loving affection," Easterngate replied. "But I'm afraid that you might not be able to recognize me when day dawns."

"She can certainly recognize you," Jin put in. "But she might not be willing to marry you after she finds out who you are."

"How could you say that!" Ma protested. "Well, let me clean myself and I'll rise and light the lamp to resume our talk."

"Don't get up," said Jin. "Just embrace each other as you do now and I'll call Axiu to kindle the light."

Axiu, disturbed by the noise of their intercourse, had not quite fallen asleep. When she heard her mistress calling, she rushed to build a fire and applied it to the lamp. During this time Easterngate did not stop kissing Ma for a minute, with his limp penis inside her, rubbing here and there from time to time.

"Are you capable of 'a-string-of-beads' combat?"[23] Jin asked.

"Of course," Easterngate said.

He ground his crotch against Ma's until he achieved erection again.

"Sister," said Ma, "am I like a starving eagle whose tummy is hard to fill up? With people being present, I'm always very prudish. But now I do not have the least scruples. I'll let my husband do whatever he likes!"

She was talking with gusto when Axiu came in, with the lamp in hand. As the bed curtain was pulled aside, Ma found, to her great surprise, that it was none other than Easterngate who was sleeping with her! Her face flushed red all over with shame.

"Sister," she said, trying to put on an air of cheerfulness, "you took me in with such a hoax!"

"So what?" Jin returned. "How could you not discover that he was my husband until after I shed light on him? You two prattled a long time and you didn't even detect his voice?"

"I was so excited," said Ma, "that I hardly paid attention to that kind of thing."

"You said you'll be my wife," Easterngate broke in, "so no more arguing!"

He went on working on her.

"How could the two of you contrive such a scheme to corrupt my virtue?" Ma grumbled. "Well, well, I now have no choice but let to you screw me as much as you like. It is just that I really don't understand why you are doing this thing to me?"

"You are pretty, that is the reason," Easterngate replied.

"No, that can't be true!" Ma refuted it. "You must tell me your real motivation!"

"You know what," Jin barged in, "it was your son who fucked me first, to begin with. He used drugs and fucked me a whole day and a whole night until he ripped my cunt apart. I hated him. That's why I tricked you with this hoax so that my husband can fuck back for me."

Ma burst into laughter. "Oh my! I never knew that the beast has a prowess that outshines even his ancestor's! It's just that he's got his old mother very much in trouble now. The wife of the Yao household was laid by my son, and now the mother of the Zhao family is being screwed by the man of the Yaos! What scandalous liaisons we are involved in! We can't but keep our mouths shut."

Easterngate pulled out his flaccid prick and wiped it clean.

"Time to sleep," Jin said.

The three of them, sharing the pillow together, dropped off.

Since then, copulating with Ma first and then with Jin, during the day or by night, had become a daily routine for Easterngate. Certainly he was very happy, though quite often he felt too exhausted to stand the strain. With her desire growing increasingly violent, Ma sometimes thought Jin troublesome in sharing pleasures with her. But Jin was not jealous as much about her own husband and his new woman being of one heart and one mind.

Coupling with these two loose women every day, Easterngate began to feel bored. He thought: Saihong's pussy, having served Dali already, will no doubt find my cock smaller than ever. To steal her actually won't give me much pleasure. Axiu the slave girl was not too bad and I used to be pretty fond of her. But now her maidenhead has been broken with Dali's debauchery, leaving my love of her much overshadowed by my resentment. Not a suitable partner either! Only Little Pretty, the maid whom Ma brought over with her, is a good-looking girl quite to my liking. Better steal her before Dali opens her hymen, so that I can taste a fresh flavour. To cast aside the overcooked steaks and pick up some bird's nest or shark's fin to eat is surely nicer, isn't it? Ma can be a problem, though. She always keeps an eye on her Little Pretty for fear of my seducing her and having therefore less energy left for herself. How should I cope with her? I must think up a method by which to keep her in the dark.

Little Pretty — let's now tell something about her — was a twelve- or thirteen-year-old who was quite big of stature and looked rather bewitching. Frequently she would become astir either to hear Easterngate and Ma making merry at night or to see Easterngate producing his member, as though it were a flute, for the two women to play with. Whenever possible, she would ask Saihong or Axiu what Master did with her mistress and why they let out delightful screams, and their detailed explanations made her feel all the more excited. However, she was very afraid of her matron's beatings and did not ever dare approach Easterngate.

One day she rose early. Hearing Easterngate lying in

bed saying he wanted a urinal, she took one from outside and brought it in for him. Easterngate pulled her to him and smacked a kiss on her mouth, at which she split with a cackle. At that time Ma and Jin were combing their hair in front of the window, chattering with each other, so they did not hear the laughter. After having finished with dressing their hair, they, hand in hand, went out to take a walk.

Easterngate got up, and before washing his face, asked Little Pretty to roll up his sleeves for him. Taking advantage of this opportunity, he let his hand go into her clothes and then reached down for her pussy. It felt like something of an iron cake, solid and somewhat round. He gave it a hard pinch, making the maid burst out squealing. Axiu hurried over at once upon hearing the cries, asking what was happening.

"I stepped on her foot," said Easterngate.

The thing between them was thus covered up.

It was not long before Jin came in, along with Ma, and they dragged Easterngate to the small veranda for eating breakfast. Ma seated herself on Easterngate's lap, and then lifting her thin skirt, buried his cock inside her before starting her *petit déjeuner*. She remained sitting like that until they had finished the meal. Then, she opened her snatch, inviting Easterngate to feel the patch of hair. Easterngate did as he was asked, only to find it heavily drenched by her fluid, which flowed onto his hand as he touched it. At her urging, he had to force himself to lick it up, his face scrunched. When they became passionate, they went back to the bedroom and united themselves once again in intercourse. Easterngate had taken a *hajie* pill [his aphrodisiac] on an empty stomach earlier in the morning and this time successfully kept his jism in without spilling one single drop for about half a day. Jin felt rather snubbed, seeing Ma sticking closely to her husband with no intention of letting her share pleasures. She got out of bed, on the pretext of going to eat lunch. Easterngate was only too anxious to take a break for himself, so he arose too.

Now the three of them, all sitting at a table, began drinking together, laughing and joking with each other at the same time.

"Usually we drink without being able to enjoy much fun," said Easterngate. "Today I propose that we go on an alcoholic spree until we get royally drunk!"

"As you say," Jin responded, seeing him mumbling something like a jingle.

"I have no objection," Ma agreed too.

Easterngate, having drained a cup of wine, took the initiative with the following tongue-twister:

> Banana, banana,
> Big leaves but no flower.
> Downed by a frosty shower,
> Like a lotus in the West Lake's water,
> In Qiantang, Zhejiang, during our Great Ming's
> Power,
> On the continent called Nanzhanbower.[24]
> Or perhaps more like a worn-out kasaya,
> Draped on an old friar,
> Sitting nearby the west veranda,
> Behind the bright black barrier,
> In the Temple of Calm's bower.

"I can't repeat it," Jin said.

"Well," Easterngate compromised, "I allow you to pause three times."

"Too many words to remember!" Ma protested.

Easterngate had to recite it several times.

"Now I can," Jin declared.

But no sooner had she started than she made a mistake and she redid it ten more times and drank ten forfeit cups. Ma only distorted two lines, so she drank two half-forfeit cups.

"I have a good rhyme, too," said Jin. "I'll sing the song first before giving you the tongue-twister."

"Go ahead!" Easterngate pressed.

Jin tossed down a cup first and then started:

> The moon, crescent, shines its light upon the Nine States,[25]
> How many of good cheer, how many remain unfortunate?
> How many sit in lofty towers, sipping good champagne?
> How many wander destitute, carrying a load, in foreign states?
>
> Downstairs, tethered an ox,
> Upstairs, lies a pail of oil.
> The shed crushes with the pulling of the ox
> And the ox is killed by the pail of oil.
> The peddler of oil, tears in eyes, cannot but sob,
> Getting the oxhide paid for his shed, its fat for oil.

"Sounds very familiar," said Easterngate.

He reproduced it at one go without making the slightest error. He then quaffed a cup of wine placed before him. Ma, unable to recall all the lines, repeated five or six times before getting the whole ballad right. She had to drink a full cup as a forfeit.

"You both have created a tongue-twister," she said, "but don't think I can't!"

"Say whatever you like," Easterngate encouraged her.

She finished her remaining half cup before piping up her creation:

> There is a bumblebee that fears wind,
> And a honeybee that does not fear wind.
> Hiding in the wall is the bumblebee fearing wind,
> Yet the honeybee comes pulling it, braving the wind.
> "I am hiding in the wall because of the wind,"
> Says the bumblebee fearing wind.
> "How can you drag me out into the wind,
> Just because you are not so afraid of wind?"[26]

"Bravo!" Easterngate exclaimed.

When he repeated it, however, he erred in three or four places and had to drink three or four cupfuls as a forfeit. Jin made even more blunders and drank five or six forfeit cups. Easterngate thanked Ma for her tongue-twister and urged her to drink a toast in return, which she declined over and over again but without success, and finally had to gulp down a full cup. She was not a good drinker. So much wine had she imbibed that she was very tiddly now.

"Today," said Easterngate, "I'll make everyone happy!"

He called Saihong, Axiu, and Little Pretty to come over.

"I'll grant each of you three cups of wine!" he said.

Complying with his proposal, Saihong and Axiu both emptied their portion. Little Pretty, however, adamantly refused to take hers.

"No, I really can't, not even a drop," she said.

"All right," said Easterngate, "I let you off."

He then, once again, urged Jin. Since she was tipsy already, she could not hold out against his pressing and quaffed another three or four cups.

"I'm afraid I have to go to bed now," she said. "If I stagger on here, I'll throw up."

"I'm drunk, too," Ma mumbled, "and I have a bad headache, feeling as if I were a mill rotating on and on." So saying, she tumbled into bed and soon fell asleep.

Saihong and Axiu were both very muddled, lying on the floor and having no energy to clear away the plates and cups on the table. Seeing them all drunk, Little Pretty could not help laughing.

What a fabulous scheme! thought Easterngate. Now that the entire family is nappy, she has nobody to be afraid of any more.

With one pull he took Little Pretty into his arms, his tipsiness giving him an unusual strength. The potency of the *hajie* pill that he had taken earlier was still laying hold of him and he dashed madly at her, trying to make a way in. Little Pretty, fearing pain, struggled desperately.

"Look," cooed Easterngate, "your matron is dead drunk! Since you'll be laid by Mr. Zhao sooner or later, you'd better let me do it now. My thing is smaller, its tip pointed and the shaft shorter, so it won't cause you much pain. Actually it can ready you for his huge rod and make you suffer less."

Little Pretty tried to push him aside with a violent shove, but Easterngate clutched her tightly. At length, he succeeded in carrying her to the bed. After laying her down and removing her lower garments, he wiped some spit on her pussy and slowly impaled her with himself.

"Oh, it hurts!" she let out a loud cry. "Go slower please! And be gentler!"

Easterngate slowed down his proceedings at her entreaties. After sticking it in, he began thrusting in a manner just as mild, and thrust into her about two hundred times till he ejaculated. Then both of them fell into sleep, folding each other in embrace.

Who would have thought that Saihong had awakened. She came into the bedroom and strode to the bedside, giving Little Pretty three or four punches on the thigh. Little Pretty jumped up before realizing who it was.

"Help!" she screamed.

Her cry startled Easterngate and he jumped up too.

"Who is it?" he asked.

"Little fox!" cursed Saihong. "You dared do such a thing! When your mistress wakes up, I'll see if she'll not beat your brains out!"

Little Pretty did not dare answer back.

"Well, well," Easterngate interposed. "For my sake, please don't fight any more, lest she awaken and lash into fury."

He then grabbed hold of Saihong and said, placating, "I'll make it with you, all right?"

This was exactly what she wanted, so she did not reject him as he pulled down her pants. Easterngate had just spent and could not harden quickly enough, very much the same quandary that he had been in the last time when he returned from the outer study to the bedroom, with a weak penis. He drew up his forces in the hope of stuffing it in, and no sooner had it turned semi-hard than he straightened his back and ground his way, in jerky gyrations, up her vagina.

Saihong laughed. "How can such a thing screw me?"

But it became stiff at last and Easterngate, without delay, started his attack. Fortunately, it remained firm throughout. Little Pretty put on her drawers and skirt and supported Saihong with her hands so that she would not fall off the bed while sitting on its edge enjoying pleasure. However, she had hardly received fifty strokes or so when Jin suddenly woke up. Sitting up, she caught sight of them in no time in the midst of copulation.

"Bitchy slave," she yelled, "how dare you do such a thing!"

Flurried, Easterngate pulled himself out as quickly as he could before Jin jumped off the bed and rushed to the maid, grabbing her ear with one hand and with the other giving her two loud slaps on the face.

"Who gave you the permission to be so damn bold?" she roared.

She then turned to Easterngate and hurled abuse at him: "Asshole! You can't even handle the women in your hands and yet you'd have the brass to toy with ill-gotten gains!"

Ma was awakened by the loud swearing.

"What's happening?" she asked.

"Can you believe," Jin complained to her, "that while we were sleeping, she would have dared take liberties as daringly as a floozie!"

Ma doubted that she meant Little Pretty.

"Was Little Pretty involved in the revelry?" she asked Axiu.

"Yes, it was she who first made love with Master," Axiu

replied. "Saihong just followed suit when she seized a chance for herself. But she was seen by Mother, unfortunately."

Ma flew into a rage upon hearing this.

"I could never conceive the notion that this little cunny could be so consumed with lustful desire!"

Allowing no time for the maid to defend herself, Ma seized her and gave her a good beating, the violent punishment sending the ornaments and decorations on the table all over the room, broken. Little Pretty did not dare utter a word.

Easterngate snickered. "It's I who hugged them and forced them into playing with me," he said. "So please don't make a fuss any more!"

The tumult thus subsided.

That night Easterngate knelt down begging his women for mercy, and it almost cost him his life to obtain their forgiveness and regain peace in the household.

One day Jin said to Ma, "You have my husband in your possession all day long and make love with him as often as you want. I have virtually been deprived of my monogamous life! Besides, you are jealous of me and I of you and both of us wish to have a man endowed with twin cocks like an eagle!"

"I have a good solution to this," Ma said to Easterngate. "You know I am only three years older than you, and Sister is only three years older than my son. So why not write a letter to my son asking him to hurry back so that I can marry you and my son can take Sister as his wife and the whole family can live together happily? What do you think of this idea?"

Jin protested, "I hate him for having been so vicious to me. Why should I let him ravish me again?"

"You shouldn't be too particular about these trifling things," Ma said. "You can still do it with Easterngate, and Dali will just be your nominal husband for the sake of camouflage. Let no one find out the real relations between us and we can continue to enjoy as much pleasure as we do now. Make sure no one will file a legal complaint against us; otherwise we'll end up in a bad scenario. To put my idea into effect is quite simple: just write a letter to Dali urging him to come back, and upon his arrival, tell him that we are going to form two new couples to live together."

Easterngate and Jin both agreed.

"Marvellous idea!" they exclaimed in chorus.

Easterngate wrote a letter right away and had it sent to his Younger Brother, who, after receiving it, took leave of his employer and returned home at once. He reported in to Ma first before going to see Easterngate and Jin.

He asked his mother, "What did you want me to come home for?"

"There is something I have to tell you, in view of the present circumstances," Ma said. She then told him everything, in great detail, about what Easterngate and Jin had done with her.

"Now," she pronounced, "I'm going to become the wife of Mr. Yao and you the husband of Mrs. Yao, and all of us will live together in harmony as one family. But mind you don't tell anybody about this!"

"Wonderful! Wonderful!" said Jin and Easterngate.

Dali, grouchy as he was, had to put up with his mother's arrangements.

"I obey you, Mom," he said.

"Now go to your bedroom and have a chat with your wife," Ma told him.

No sooner had Dali and Jin gone into their room than they kissed each other. A bustling melee ensued at once.

Easterngate said to Ma, "They are scoring. We should go enjoy ourselves as well!" Their coupling, however, did not last long. When Easterngate came out, passing by Dali's room, he saw the two of them still intertwined in bed. He sneaked in, undoing his pants and pulling out his dick all the way along.

Dali, seeing Easterngate coming for him, gruntled, "You have just screwed my mother and now you want to work on me!"

"Just for today," he insisted. "I won't bother you once more in the next few days."

"But why not do it tomorrow?" Dali grumbled.

He was on top of Jin, thrusting into her. Now Easterngate climbed onto his back and began diddling him. "This is called 'keeping-on-good-terms-with-everybody,'" he said.

They made love in threesome for some time.

Soon Easterngate got off the bed and left. When it was time for lunch, Jin and Dali came out and ate a meal together in the hall. Easterngate told Ma that he had been invited for dinner at a friend's house, and with this excuse, took leave of her. No sooner had the sun set than he returned home and crept into Jin's bedroom.

He saw Saihong had prepared a tub of hot water and placed it in the center of the room. Dali washed Jin's pussy for her and Jin bathed his buttocks for him. When they both finished, the maid handed them towels to dry themselves on. Jin then bade Saihong pour them wine. After a few cups, they were in high spirits. On the table, which usually held musical instruments, was laid fresh sea cucumber,[27] along with a steaming hot laver soup that had just now been ladled out. Saihong was standing to the side waiting upon them, a pot of well-known Yangzhou *xiangfan* liquor in hand. Jin burst out chuckling as she saw the laver.

"Why are you laughing?" Dali asked.

"You may want to use the laver later this evening," she said.

"Not tonight," said Dali. "Junior as I am, I'm also a 'swordsman' and may not need it today. But I wonder how come Yutao could impart the knowledge to you in such an explicit way?"

Jin pointed at Easterngate, explaining: "Three years ago, when he was away from home, I saw two singers wearing long hair sitting on the threshold of our gate. Since they looked very pretty, like girls, I asked them where they were from and why they sat here. They answered, 'We are from Ningbo of Zhejiang and are on our way to the Capital.' 'But you are very young and I wonder what you are going to the Capital for,' I asked. 'For serving our apprenticeship in singing, and also for making money by offering our bottoms for sale,' came their reply. The one called Yutao then told me something of the tricks he had been taught at home, and the other day, when you had anal sex with me, I applied his method, which indeed prevented filthy stuff from coming out. It works wonderfully!"

After hearing this, Dali said to Easterngate, "I'll lean over the bench to let you insert some into my hole, if you don't wish to get my unclean excreta."

Jin began her self-stuffing, too.

"I'll probably have no way of escaping either," she murmured to herself.

Finally there was not much laver left in the bowl and the three of them had to eat the sea cucumber only. They drained two or three pots of liquor and then undressed and went to bed, bidding Saihong to leave the light on. Jin lay down and cushioned her waist on a soft pillow, and spreading her legs, grabbed Dali's prick and guided it into her cunt, which was already very moist.

Seeing Easterngate going to straddle them, she called to stop him, "Wait a moment!" She then wiped a great deal of her oozed slippery fluid into the fissure of Dali's butt, to make the penetration easier. When Easterngate had stuck his penis inside, they began moving in unison, Dali giving a thrust first and then Easterngate another, and they thrust more than a hundred times altogether.

Easterngate took a breath, saying, "We are now playing *Romance of the Western Chamber*."

"What has made you think so?" Dali asked.

"Aren't we like its characters Monk Facong and his disciple Die Mopeng?"

They burst out laughing.

Easterngate asked Jin, "Is it fun?"

"Of course!" she said. "It's just that you are weighing too heavy on me."

"With me pressing on the top, your cunt can take more solid thrusts," teased Easterngate.

"We two are connected, skin to skin and flesh to flesh, but you are detached," Jin griped. "Excuse me," she said to Dali as she reached out for Easterngate's head. She kissed him on the mouth and sucked his tongue again and again.

"Now the top is linked," Easterngate quipped, "but the lower part is still not."

"I have an idea," Jin said. "But I must solicit the consent of my sweetheart first."

"You are a couple," Dali responded, "so you needn't ask for my consent."

"All right, just pull your cock out for the time being," Jin told him.

She instructed him to lie on his back underneath her, and then straddled him and put his prick inside her before inviting Easterngate to lie prone on her back and impale her anus.

"Sweetheart Yao," she said, "you have never screwed me in the asshole and today I'll let you have a try."

Easterngate laughed. "Now we are playing *Washing Silk*,"[28] he said.

"How so?" Dali asked.

"Isn't this what the King of the Wu descibes in a song he sings as he travels in Suzhou, 'Look, I am having my attendants surrounding me all around?'"

They burst out laughing again. Dali spat some spit on his fingers and rubbed it into Jin's bung, and when it was slippery enough, helped Easterngate to stuff his cock in.

"How do you feel?" Jin asked him.

"Good," he replied. "But it's a pity my johnson is not big enough to pull out your rectal tube."

They laughed and poked fun while moving harmoniously.

After fifty or sixty strokes, Easterngate said, "I feel tingly and am about to come."

"Into this mucky place? The place that can't conceive?" Jin protested. "Why are you going to spend to no purpose at all? You are not teasing me, are you? I once saw an erotic picture about the two brothers of the Zhangs making love with Empress Wu[29] in a way as if they they were sitting for the same examination and passed at the same time. You two are good brothers, and happen to be taking the same 'examination,' so why not treat me as Empress Wu by imitating what the Zhang brothers did to her?"

She then asked Dali to pull halfway out and let Easterngate halfway in. She said to Dali, "Make some space for him so that he can spend inside too. Isn't this good for both of you? If you ejaculate together and I get pregnant, it's likely that I'll give birth to twin sons. I'd then have one of them adopt the surname Yao and the other the surname Zhao and I'll be the matriarch for both families!"

Dali and Easterngate, following her instruction, let themselves be manipulated till both of their cocks had been squeezed into her twat, which was thus drawn to a considerable extent.

Jin laughed. "Ever since we had pussies in the world, has there been any woman making love with both her old husband and new husband at the same time? It is true that Empress Wu had the Zhang brothers sleeping with her, but they did it simply because they loved their official positions, not her. How can they be compared to my two husbands who are screwing me with real loving affection? What a wondrous thing!"

The three of them squirmed and rubbed each other until both men reached their orgasm and were about to come. They jerked simultaneously, so forcefully that Jin felt a tingle of pleasure racing all over her.

She cried, "I'm coming!"

In spite of herself she wriggled, having an unbearable itch inside her pelvis. Though this twitch of hers was not so violent as the buckings she had just felt, it caused the joint right above her anus to split, producing a pop.

"Oh, my goodness!" she blurted. "Both sides of the joint have been split!"

Easterngate and Dali were both in the midst of ejaculating. They had to withdraw themselves. Out came her blood-mixed essence, followed by their semen, streaming out. They flooded her front gate and her rear entrance as well as the narrow juncture in between, like pulp spilling from a bowl or porridge from a pot. The three of them all received a splash, thus having a soggy mess on their bodies.

Easterngate and Dali were taken aback as they saw the fluid. "How is it that the color is like this?" they wondered, giggling, and they ended doubling up with laughter.

Jin held her tears back, forcing herself to put on an air of cheerfulness.

"Today," she said, "I'm aching so much as if I were giving birth to a son. If I do have a son later, it is worth the pain; but if not, you two should each make yourself be a fine son and call me Mother."

They laughed.

"Well, let me snuggle down and nurse my injuries," she said, wiping off the blood and semen lightly. Both men then separated and slept at her either side.

Our story goes that Ma had been lying in bed waiting for Easterngate, with the door of her bedroom left ajar. There was, however, no sign of his returning. All of sudden, in a drowsy state, she heard laughter coming from the other chamber. She called Little Pretty to go there and take a look.

Little Pretty came back and reported to her: "Master is playing with Aunt Jin."

Upon hearing this, Ma didn't even allow herself time to ask what Dali was doing there. She rushed to their room wearing just a skirt of thin silk and a sleeveless unlined upper garment, the fabric of which was transparent.

She yelled at Easterngate: "What time is it now? And what makes you so willing to hang on here and refuse to clear out?"

She then turned to Jin and swore, "Shameless hussy! You have got a man already, why do you want another one, huh?"

Jin was provoked.

"Shame on you, old cuss!" she fired back "You have the nerve to curse me! He is not your legal husband and what right do you have to take possession of him all to yourself?"

Ma took umbrage and started to cry. "Impubic seductress! Crooked wanton! How daring you are to take such liberties!" She swore while wailing, and then seizing Easterngate, beat him ferociously.

"You heartless son of bitch! You allow her to curse me?"

Easterngate did not dare utter a word and let her strike him.

"You heartless son of bitch!" she wept even more loudly. "How can you let your ex-wife curse me like this?"

Dali, fearing the loud noise his mother was making, had to intervene.

"Mom, stop it please! The things we have been doing are disgraceful and if our neighbours figure out the real situation in our household, we'll sure court a rebutt."

"Now you have beaten me enough," said Easterngate, "I beg you to calm down, please!"

He reached out and took Ma into his arms, and after having said every fine word he could, finally succeeded in persuading her to go back to their own room. Ma was still in tears and Easterngate had to harden his phallus to cringe to her. But no matter how he tried, she remained sullen.

The next morning Jin got up, dejected. In the company of Dali, she went over to her mother-in-law and apologized: "The daughter-in-law offended Mother yesterday and she is now willing to be punished as you please."

Ma broke into a smile.

Yet the neighbors had already caught wind of their quarrel.

"What outrageous things they did!" they commented.

At that time the Commissioner for Education happened to be making an inspection tour in Yangzhou and two or three scholar-lords denounced Yao Tongxin and Zhao Dali to him for their inappropriate behaviour. The news frightened Dali. He came back home and consulted with Jin and Ma. With the approval of Easterngate, the whole family then fled to Mount Yetui to take refuge, where they built for themselves a small house with six or seven rooms and lived a free and happy life together.

By then Ma was three months pregnant. She bore Easterngate two sons and lived joyfully with him for three years. Because of her frequent intercourse in the first month after giving birth, she caught postnatal infection and died. Jin was oversexed as before and her excessive lovemaking inevitably resulted in disorders of her womb, making her unable to conceive a child any more. As she grew weaker and weaker, she forced Dali to couple with her by day and by night and at last, her marrow ran dry. She died from sex-related exhaustion at the age of twenty-four. Saihong and Axiu both married, but they were soon sold by their husbands to prostitution. Only Little Pretty, raising the two sons by Ma, went on living in the mountains alone.

Dali was disquieted, often pestered by Jin in his dreams. He consulted with Easterngate: "We are lonely living here by ourselves. It might be better to go somewhere else and register at a residential school there."

"This is a good idea," Easterngate agreed.

They left for Beijing. Some fellow townsmen there had already spread their scandals and there was not one who did not regard them as beasts or liked to make their acquaintances. They had to pack up and come back. On their return trip, however, Dali caught pestilence when they stopped in Dezhou and was all of sudden taken by death. Easterngate cried his eyes out over his decease.

"My good brother!" he wailed, "with you dead, my wife dead, I now have only a broken family left to me!"

He cremated Dali's corpse, and after having packed the bones and ashes, returned to the mountains. Seeing Little Pretty wearing an unhappy look all day long, he was in no mood to make merry with her any more. One day, at noon, he felt rather depressed and dozed off against a table. Suddenly, in his dream, he saw a sow, a male mule, and a female mule approaching him. He was startled.

"Who are you?" he asked.

"I am Ma," answered the sow, like a human being.

"I am Jin," answered the female mule.

"I am Dali," answered the male mule.

"But why have you all come here?" he asked.

The sow replied, "The King of Yama blamed me for having lost my chastity and bearing illegitimate sons, so he punished me by changing me into a female pig so that I shall always have labour pains."

The female mule replied, "The King of Yama blamed me for my sexual indulgence, especially my entanglement with a lover." After a pause, she added, "Since my dissipation had something to do with Dali's large cock, both of us have been transformed into mules as punishment. Being a female mule, I am very lecherous, but I can't have sex any more, while the male mule, endowed as he is with a huge penis, has not been allowed to come together with me, even once."

The male mule replied, "I have suffered awfully. I have to rush back and forth on the road all the time and have not ever had a chance again to enjoy pleasures with her. My mother has longed for you very much, so today, at her request, we all came to see you in your dream."

Easterngate was greatly surprised.

"Can I be pardoned?" he asked, crying.

The male mule replied, "The other day I inquired about your case in the nether world and was told that since you indulged your wife in keeping a lover, you'll be reincarnated into a turtle. That is the punishment you will receive. But I argued for you at the risk of my life: 'It was simply our fault and had nothing to do with him. My bones and ashes, thanks to his kindness, were taken back home by him.' This was an enormous good deed you have done without others' knowledge. The judge then checked about it in his register, and before running through all the pages, did see the record of your taking back my bones and ashes. He said, 'You three all lived off him. I am afraid you owe him too much to pay him back.' Maybe only after you kill the sow and ride us two mules will we be able to repay our debts."

A cold wind blew over and the three animals disappeared. Easterngate gave out a loud cry, only to wake himself up and find that it was a dream.

He sighed, "It seems that there indeed is the law of retribution. The sufferer never knows anything but hardship, injury leads to injury, and good comes to good. When will the end of all this arrive?"

He sneaked back to his old house, and taking some silver with him, went to the Temple of Emptiness, where in front of some Buddhist masters of high attainment he confessed all the sins the three of them had committed. Afterward, on a selected day, he wedded Little Pretty to a comely youth from an ordinary family, to whom he also entrusted his two sons by Ma. He himself never again rode a mule nor ate pork.

One day Ma, Jin, and Dali appeared in his dream once again.

"Many thanks for your confession," they said. "Now we are not so sinful as before and maybe soon we'll be reincarnated as humans."

Easterngate was very glad to hear that.

He said to himself, "What about myself? I'm still iniquitous!"

He then took tonsure, and wearing a *kasaya*, went to the Temple of Emptiness to join the Buddhist order as a novice. He gave himself an ecclesiastic name, "Xi Zhu" [West Indian] and people simply called him "Monk Zhu." He spent all his time in the temple reading sutras and practising abstinence from eating meat. On an empty spot within the church premises he built for himself a small shrine, on the wall of which he hung a plate with four big characters: *Mo Deng Luo Cha* [Matan Raksasa].[30] These four words came from a Buddhist scripture and only those who had read the text would know the real meaning of the phrase. Now that he had cleared his mind and achieved enlightenment, he was finally able to enjoy its fructification.

He then often told people his own story, to give them some well-meaning advice for being good. An interested listener, therefore, wrote a short romance for him that was based on his recounting. Some readers laughed at him after reading the story, while others condemned him. Certainly he is a character worth being commented on.

This is the end of the tale. Gu Fanglai[31] remarks: "Good! Easterngate ended up as a penitent, so he made himself different from the other three sinners."

Some might say, "Ma, Jin, and Zhao were beasts indeed, but the discourser has also been guilty of disseminating this story. What do you think?"

Fanglai replies, "The story is based on facts, with which the discourser intended to admonish the world, so what guilt does he have?"

Yao-Zhao the two pricks are as crazy
As Ma-Jin the pair of licentious pussies.
Axiu and Saihong both part company,
To the end remains only Little Pretty.

The pig and mules are their reincarnation,
Retribution does indeed have its regulation.
No family, sons, suffering ne'er ceasing,
What a taste of this endless condemnation!

— to the tune of *The Moon on the Western River*[32]

NOTES

[1] Cangwurao (or Cangwu) was a contemporary of Confucius.

[2] Chen Ping (?-178 BC) was a prime minister in the Han dynasty. When he was young he had an affair with his elder brother's wife.

[3] Changzhou was a town very close to Yangzhou.

[4] The units of measurement of ancient China, such as "inch" mentioned here, were usually shorter than their current equivalents.

[5] Xue Aocao is the main character in the Ming erotic story *Ruyi jun zhuan* (Story of the Lord of Perfect Satisfaction), who had a huge penis.

[6] Ji Bu was a knight-errant in the Han dynasty, so famous for honoring his word that people at the time believed that to obtain his promise was better than having a thousand pieces of gold.

[7] Washing one's feet usually included washing one's privates, and this custom did not change much even in the twentieth century when most people still could not take a bath every day.

[8] "Little mother" (*xiaoniang*) in Chinese is "courtesan."

[9] Luo Longwen (?-1567), was an aide to Yan Shifan (?-1567), Minister of Work in the late Jiajing reign. Luo served Yan as his secretary and took bribes for him. He was one of Yan's most corrupt men (see *Ming shi*, "Biography of Zou Yinglong," vol. 18, p. 5569) and was executed in 1567.

[10] This is a punning allusion. In history the Song court was defeated by the Jin (Jurchen, or Nuzhen) and was driven to the south, where, in Lin'an (modern Hangzhou), they established the Southern Song court.

[11] Cui refers to Cui Yingying (Oriole), the heroine in the famous play *Xixiang ji* (Romance of the Western Chamber), with whom Scholar Zhang longs to have a love affair.

[12] Emperor Huizong and Emperor Qinzong were the last two emperors of the Northern Song dynasty, who were captured by the Jin and died as their captives in Northeast China.

[13] This is an historical allusion. Ma Su, a high-ranking military officer of the Shu in the Three-Kingdoms period (220-280) took his enemy lightly and therefore lost an important strategic point, Jieting, in his battle with the army of the Wei.

[14] This is also an historical allusion, referring to Zhuge Liang, a well-known strategist of the Shu who presented a woman's headdress to Sima Yi, the general of the army of the Wei, in order to enrage him and force him to fight to the finish when his army was on the defensive, reluctant to contend against its opponent.

[15] One of the major minorities in China.

[16] Men's garments at that time did not have pockets. Small things were usually carried inside their long, wide sleeves.

[17] Guazhou is a small town, very close to Yangzhou.

[18] Qiu Shizhou was an alias of Qiu Ying (?-1552), a Ming artist well-known for his erotic paintings.

[19] Ma Lanxiang, usually written as Ma Xianglan, was a famous courtesan in Nanjiang, active in the middle of Wanli reign (around 1600). She was a fine poet and also good at painting bamboo. She has left two volumes of poetry, posthumously published by her lover surnamed Wang in the Wanli reign.

[20] It is obvious that "Prince of Yue" alludes to the Prince of Fujian, Changxun (1582-1642), the second but most favorite son of Emperor Shenzong (c. 1573-1619), who did not make his eldest son Changluo heir apparent until the twenty-ninth year of the Wanli reign (1601). It was rumoured that the Emperor wanted Changxun to succeed him, indulging him by spending more than a half million, ten times as much as was usually allowed, on his wedding and on the building of a luxurious residence on his enfeoffment in Luoyang. Hence the nickname "The Transgressive Young Man of the Proprieties." For details, see *Ming shi* (History of the Ming), pps. 293-94, 3649-50, and 6233 (Beijing: Zhonghua shuju, 1974).

[21] Huzhou was a town in Zhejiang province, located on the other side of Lake Tai. To get there from Yangzhou at the time one needed to go by boat and the journey would take several days.

[22] Around 11 o'clock.

[23] One sexual bout after another, without much rest after ejaculation.

[24] This name, I gather, is made up by Easterngate. I have slightly altered the last syllable in my transliteration in order to make it fit the rhyme.

[25] "The Nine States" refers to China, which used to be divided into nine administrative regions.

[26] Here I will copy out one of the retranslations of these three tongue-twisters by Professor Wendy Larson, for readers' appreciation:

> *There's a wind-fearing bumblebee*
> *And a wind-not-fearing honeybee.*
> *The wind-fearing bumblebee*
> *Hides in the wall so furtively.*
> *The wind-not-fearing honeybee*
> *Pulls it out quite heartlessly.*
> *Scolding the wind-not-fearing honeybee,*
> *The wind-fearing bumblebee*
> *Says, how can you drag me out so heedlessly*
> *Just because you're so fear-free?*

[27] "Sea cucumber" in the original text is "hai bi rou," literally meaning "meat of sea cunt." I do not know for sure what kind of meat this is exactly and my translation might be incorrect. (Someone suggests it could be sea horse, which is very good for strengthening sexual power.)

[28] *Washing Silk* (Huansha ji) is a Ming play written by Liang Chenyu. It tells the story of the rise and decline of the States Wu and Yue in the Warring States period.

[29] The two Zhang brothers were both Empress Wu's lovers. Their story, elaborated in *Story of the Lord of Perfect Satisfaction*, seems to have been quite popular in the Ming dynasty.

[30] Lecherous devil.

[31] This is a metaphorical name, meaning "not far from ancient times."

[32] In fact, this is a septasyllabic regulated verse, not a lyric (*ci*) written to the tune *The Moon on the Western River.*

AUTHOR & TRANSLATOR

Born in Shanghai, Lenny L. Hu received his higher education in China and in the United States. He came to Canada in 1988 to attend the University of British Columbia and then the University of Toronto, where he earned his Ph.D. He has translated American writer Philip Roth's novel *Goodbye, Columbus* and some other English literary works into Chinese. Currently he teaches at the University of Toronto.